PUFFIN BOOKS

Children's WARD

THE CRASH

Children's WARD

THE CRASH

Helen White

from the Granada Television series
created by Paul Abbot and Kay Mellor

PUFFIN BOOKS

PUFFIN BOOKS

Published by the Penguin Group
Penguin Books Ltd, 27 Wrights Lane, London W8 5TZ, England
Penguin Books USA Inc., 375 Hudson Street, New York, New York 10014, USA
Penguin Books Australia Ltd, Ringwood, Victoria, Australia
Penguin Books Canada Ltd, 10 Alcorn Avenue, Toronto, Ontario, Canada M4V 3B2
Penguin Books (NZ) Ltd, 182–190 Wairau Road, Auckland 10, New Zealand

Penguin Books Ltd, Registered Offices: Harmondsworth, Middlesex, England

First published in Puffin Books 1994
1 3 5 7 9 10 8 6 4 2

Typeset by Datix International Limited, Bungay, Suffolk
Printed in England by Clays Ltd, St Ives plc

One

The gang were hanging out in the precinct.

Phil was restless. At twelve he was three years younger than the others, but Jude always let him tag along.

'So what we doing, then?' he challenged. 'Nothing?' Nowadays all that the others seemed to want to do was sit around in couples, smoking and swigging cider. They needed a laugh. Jude was good for a laugh, but ever since he'd been going out with Faye, he'd been a lot less fun.

Tall Jude settled more comfortably on the wall. He flicked his floppy fair hair and grinned his famous grin at Phil. Then, spreading his arms in mock puzzlement, he asked: 'Why's everyone looking at me?'

He surveyed them, all waiting for his decision: Faye, with her straggly long blonde hair; sallow-faced Dan and dark-skinned Sarah, all dressed up in the right labels and nowhere to go. And Phil, of course, eyes wide with anticipation in his dark face.

Jude stood up. 'Doesn't matter where we go as long as we go in style.' He flicked down his fag-end. 'Dan. Sarah. Get us a car.'

This was more like it. Brought to life by the command, Dan gave a demon grin and whipped out his screwdriver.

'Yesss!' hissed Phil.

Dan and Sarah went gliding along the row of parked cars.

'Ten seconds max,' Dan breathed suddenly, and dropped to his knees beside a Vauxhall Cavalier.

Sarah stood on the lookout, counting. Eight . . . nine . . . Ten seconds had gone and he had failed to beat his own record, he was still struggling with the lock.

'Hurry up!' She looked round anxiously.

'Shut it.' He was frustrated, starting to sweat.

The lock clicked undone.

Sarah catapulted into the road in relief and round to the passenger door.

Inside, Dan was barrelling the ignition. The engine took. 'Yesss!'

The car screeched away from the kerb and out of the street, heading back towards the precinct.

Back at the precinct, Faye nipped off to buy fags. She kissed Jude before she went, and Phil taunted him: 'You've gone soft. And you're never there nowadays. You weren't even there when Carl brought his brother's bike. It was a good laugh.'

Jude sneered amiably down his long nose. 'It's not such a laugh when you've done it twenty times. If you think I'm going to spend the rest of my life hanging around with this bunch of deadheads, you can think again.' He went on, half to himself: 'I've got better things to do. When school finishes . . . There'll be jobs going in the multiplex. Pay enough cash to get me out of this place.'

Phil was shocked. It had never occurred to him that Jude – of all people – could get fed up with the gang. It made Phil feel weird, kind of abandoned and betrayed.

He said roughly, only half-joking: 'What a wimp!'

And, to his relief, Jude turned on him with his usual cheerful viciousness, grabbed his arm and twisted it up behind his back.

They broke apart as Dan roared the car into the close near by. He made a screaming circle to impress, then came to a skidding halt, doors opening for them, ready.

'Wow!' cried Phil, darting across and jumping in the back.

Jude ambled over, maddeningly slow. 'Call that a car?'

'Get in, Jude!' cried Sarah, excited but on edge. 'We can't stay round here, they'll be looking.'

Jude looked towards the corner where Faye would be coming.

'Aw!' Phil taunted. 'He needs Faye to hold his hand!'

Which decided Jude. He jumped in, landing on Phil, and pummelled him.

At that moment Faye was stepping out of the newsagent's. Two girls of about ten blocked her way, intently discussing Take That. 'It's true!' ten-year-old Tanya was protesting. 'The radio said Robbie was leaving!'

Nine-year-old Debbie shook her head firmly. 'He'd never do that.'

Bickering in friendly fashion, the two girls turned along the street towards the play area, in the opposite direction to Faye.

'Which way?' Dan asked Jude. Sarah was agitating to get away, but he didn't know where to head.

'Up to you,' Jude grinned from the back, and, unable to decide, Dan went round the block yet again. They went wide round a corner, tyres squealing, and were all thrown to one side.

'Slow down!' cried Sarah.

Dan sneered: 'Chicken!'

'Slow down,' she repeated tensely. Her fists were clenched.

Phil was scrambling over them to get at the sunroof. With a whoop of triumph he pushed his top half through and yelled in exhilaration at the rush of air on his face.

As Faye reached the precinct she saw this sight: the car speeding up with Phil's torso poking up through the roof, arms wildly outstretched. They whooped at her and burned on past again.

'Go back for her!' Jude demanded. 'Turn here!'

Dan flung the wheel and turned sharply under an archway towards the play area.

Halfway across the play area, Debbie and Tanya heard the car squealing through the archway. It shot out towards them; Dan tried to turn; he lost control. In the moment before he crashed, he saw their faces quite clearly: Tanya and Debbie, straight in his path, staring in terror back through the windscreen . . . Then, in the midst of tremendous banging, everything went black.

Faye heard the sickening crash. No. It couldn't be happening. She stood quite still. Then her feet went forward, one after the other, and at last she was running. She turned the corner into the play area.

The car was wrecked, plunged into a wall. There was silence. Two young girls lay spread-eagled and unmoving. Bent double across the roof of the car, Phil was beginning to squirm. And the others? Jude? Nothing. No sound.

'Jude!' she screamed, running to the car, tugging at the buckled doors to get at the silent slumped figures inside.

It was not going to be a quiet day on Children's Ward B1 at South Park Hospital.

For Nurse Diane Gallagher it was a big day already. Her first one back at work, part-time, after having baby Dominic. What had once been normal routine now felt strange – far stranger than when she'd first started nursing. Then, everything had been simply an exciting challenge. But now she was torn between her desire to be here, back at last in the world of work, and her need to be with Dominic. She was missing him already. And worrying about him: how would he settle at the child-minder's? It wasn't so easy, she'd discovered, to cut off, divide your life into compartments, once you became a mother. And there was another thing. At one time Diane had been Sister on this ward. Leaving to have Dominic had put paid to that, and Staff Nurse Sandra Mitchell had been promoted Sister in her place. So the roles were reversed, and now Diane would have to answer to *her*. Sandra Mitchell had seldom been known to pass up a chance to play the headmistress, and Diane at this moment was feeling like a little girl starting school.

She straightened her belt, patted her blonde hair

and stepped out of the staff locker-room to face the day.

Mags, the middle-aged auxiliary nurse, didn't exactly help. 'Look at you!' she cried, catching sight of Diane in her old Staff Nurse's uniform. 'Time warp!'

Sister Mitchell bore down on them like a teacher coming to silence the naughty girls. 'I want a word, Diane, before you start.'

Diane's heart sank. 'Oh, you got my note about leaving early!' she said as brightly as she could. 'The thing is . . . it's Dominic's first day at the childminder's, and if I'm not there by five-thirty she might cross me off the list.' She cringed inwardly with guilt, and she had a horrible conviction that Sandra would now take the chance Diane was afraid she'd always been looking for: to write her off as incompetent once and for all. 'I know I'm on half-shift as it is . . . but . . . Just this once . . . ?'

Sandra's pretty but supercilious face had given not a flicker. Then: 'Fine,' she said blandly, to Diane's surprise and relief. Her snooty expression melted in a smile. 'I just wanted to say welcome back.'

Cheered, Diane went on into the bright ward, which was filled with the quiet hum of children's activity.

Here, six-year-old Heather Mason was newly

arrived for a minor operation – the removal of a mole on her shoulder which her swimsuit strap kept rubbing. Student Nurse Rob was showing Heather and her mother to her bed. She was very nervous. Her fair ponytail trembled as she looked around the ward, which to her seemed huge and awe-inspiring.

They were interrupted by a dark, lively-looking boy of about twelve who asked Rob: 'Can I change my lunch order to bacon?'

'No,' Rob replied cheerfully. He introduced the boy to Heather. 'This is Jamie. He's been here so many times, he knows this ward better than I do. An old hand.' He laughed, nodding towards Jamie's actual hand, which was swathed in bandages.

Heather stared at it in fearful awe. 'What have you done to it?' she asked.

Jamie told her matter-of-factly: 'I got it caught in a machine. I've just had another op on it. You should have seen it when I did it. Blood all over. Sliced two fingers off.'

Rob's joke, meant to put Heather at ease, had misfired. She went white, and buried her face in her mother's side, more upset than ever about coming into hospital.

Mrs Mason frowned, not at all pleased at the way things were going.

Jamie moved on to nine-year-old Ellie near by, and asked her to swap her lunch with him. Pale-faced Ellie shook her head of black hair. She wouldn't be having a lunch to swap: she was going for an X-ray on her stomach and so she wasn't allowed to eat beforehand. Ellie was a quiet girl. Without any fuss, she had quietly made herself at home on Children's Ward. The walls behind her bed were cheerful with pictures, and on her locker was a bright array of cards and fluffy toys. She'd be an encouraging example, Heather's mother thought, if only Heather would stop crying and look up.

'So what's wrong with your stomach?' Jamie asked Ellie.

'They don't know. Dr Gallagher says I'm a mystery,' she told him proudly.

Another livewire came up and joined them, a freckled boy of around the same age as Jamie: Sean Swift, or Swifty as he preferred to be called. Swifty was famously accident-prone, and as a result was even more of a regular than Jamie on Children's Ward. For once, though, he wasn't a patient. He had come with his dad, who had a reason for being here far more ominous to Swifty than anyone being ill. Six months before, when Swifty *had* been a patient, his father, Tom, and the dragon Sister Mitchell – both newly divorced – had struck up an acquaintance. The normally cheery Swifty had watched events unfolding in disbelief and dread.

'She stayed the night last Thursday,' he now told Jamie grimly.

At this rate, his worst nightmare could well be realized.

'Downer!' Jamie agreed.

Near by, Diane was stripping a bed with Student Nurse Keely Johnson, her old friend from way back – ever since the time when Diane herself had been a newly qualified nurse here and Keely a fifteen-year-old patient. Diane had been looking forward to this chance to chat.

She told Keely: 'There were tears when I left Dominic this morning.' She confessed: 'Mine.' She knew that Keely, who had little Lauren, would understand.

'Have you got a childminder?' Keely asked, and Diane didn't notice straight away that Keely's tone was a bit irritable and that her glossy dark head was bent, avoiding her gaze.

'Yes – Elaine. In Didsbury,' Diane said eagerly, and prepared to launch into all the details about her.

Keely cut in: 'Wish *I* could afford a childminder. I have to leave Lauren with my mum, and I wish I didn't have to, she smokes. But then *I* haven't got a doctor's wages to support *me*.' She saw that there were no clean pillow-slips and huffed in irritation, and she had gone to find some before Diane could utter another word.

And there, at that very moment, was Diane's husband, Dr Kieran Gallagher, appearing right at her side.

'What do you think's wrong with Keely?' she asked him in dismay.

Kieran gave his usual boyish, 'search-me' grin. 'Exams? She and Rob have got their finals in a couple of days.'

Of course! Poor Keely: a full-time job, her partner, Billy, working away in Southampton, having to cope with Lauren all on her own – and, on top of it all, the exams coming up. How on earth did she do it?

And here Diane had been, moaning about problems which didn't bear comparison. No wonder Keely had felt narked.

Kieran grinned, teasing. 'If she makes you a cup of tea, check what's in it.' And he headed off down the ward to where Heather and her mother were still waiting for him to admit her.

As he introduced himself to them, his bleep went off.

'Sorry. I'll be back as soon as I can.' He was off at a scoot.

Heather's mum was growing more dissatisfied by the minute.

The bleep had been calling him to Casualty. As he reached the ward doorway, Sister Sandra Mitchell swooped out of the office to catch him.

'Casualty have been on the phone. Six children. Joyriders. I'll get things ready up here.'

Kieran nodded, already halfway down the corridor, on his way to them.

Down in Casualty, they were wheeling in the first stretchers. On one of them Phil's dark head bobbed from side to side in protest. 'I can walk! There's nothing wrong with me!' He had managed to climb down from the car before the police and ambulances had arrived. Now he was claiming he'd never been in it, he'd been a bystander and they'd picked him up by mistake.

However, he couldn't stop himself craning around and looking for the others. All he could see at the moment was the figure lying on the nearest stretcher. It was one of the girls they'd run down. Her eyes were closed in her gashed face, and she lay quite still . . .

Where was Jude? They'd brought him, unconscious, in the same ambulance, but now Phil couldn't see him anywhere.

And the others? As if in answer, the rubber doors flapped open, and Dan and Sarah were wheeled in from the other ambulance.

Phil couldn't see their faces, but, as their trolleys veered close, he heard Dan whisper vehemently to Sarah through his pain: 'Don't tell them nothing.'

Sarah failed to reply.

Some twenty minutes later, full of trepidation, Faye

stepped through the doors of Casualty. She hadn't dared come in the ambulance. The crash scene had quickly been swarming with police, and she'd kept her distance and followed, running, to the hospital.

And now two officers were standing near the reception desk, patrolling the area she'd have to cross. Afraid but determined, she strode towards the cubicles where the stretchers must be. They didn't challenge her, and she reached the cubicles unnoticed. All the curtains were closed. She tugged the nearest one open and peeped in. A doctor was bent over a girl who lay unconscious, one of the girls who'd been lying in the road . . .

A voice came from behind another curtain. A man's voice, a doctor: 'We're not getting any response. I don't like the look of it.'

An awful dread filled her. And at that moment the doctor emerged, flicking the curtain aside, and she saw what she'd been fearing: Jude lying on the bed behind the man, eyes closed and still.

'Jude!' She rushed towards him.

The doctor caught her, gently restraining her. 'Steady on.'

'Is he all right?'

'It's too early to say. He's taken a bad knock.'

She looked at Jude's face, deathly pale but, it seemed, unmarked. 'He must be all right! Look at him!'

'Look,' Dr Gallagher said, growing a little less patient but still holding on to her arm. 'We're very busy here. If you want to help him, go to the desk. Tell them his details – we need to contact his family as soon as possible. Is that his name – Jude?'

She panicked. Names, details, and the police crawling everywhere. She looked up. The two officers were making for the cubicles.

She ran, across the foyer and out of the hospital altogether.

Up on B1 Sister Mitchell was preparing the staff for the imminent arrival of road traffic accident victims.

'Right!' she said finally. 'Let's not hang about. Most of this new intake are going to be on quarter-hour observation, and once they arrive we'll be pushed.'

The staff dispersed to their allotted tasks. Diane glanced anxiously at her watch. Only forty-five minutes before she had to collect Dominic. Yet it was hardly a situation in which a Staff Nurse should duck off early . . .

Since he seemed to be unscathed, Phil was the first to arrive on the ward. He was wheeled in still insisting that he ought to be allowed to go home. He was indignant when Sister Mitchell took his temperature. 'A little less of the amateur dramatics next time,' she told him curtly when it was done.

'Jawohl, mein Führer,' he cheeked her.

This drew the attention of Mags, the motherly

auxiliary. She stared at Phil in disbelief and recognition. 'Is that really you, Phil Murphy?' she cried, more indignant than he was. 'Eileen's boy?' She told Student Nurse Keely, who was still near by: 'I know her from down the club.' She turned back to Phil. 'How old are you, twelve? Twelve years old and caught up with that lot? What's your mother going to say? Stealing cars at your age!'

Phil rolled his eyes and looked away.

Keely touched Mags's elbow in warning, but Mags was in full flow, outraged. 'Joyriding they call it, don't they? *Joy*riding? Where's the *joy* in that, eh?' She pointed along the ward to drawn curtains, behind which the other arrivals were being settled in. 'You're lucky to get away with just a few bruises!'

'Just bog off,' Phil muttered under his breath.

Mags tutted furiously. 'I hope you're proud. This'll break your mother's heart.'

'Come on,' Keely said gently. 'Let him sleep.'

Mags shrugged her off, offended. 'Huh! Don't mind me, I'm just the hired hand! Pardon me for having opinions!' And she stalked off.

Keely left Phil in peace.

A moment later no one noticed him catch hold of his stomach and wince in pain.

Mags wasn't the only person put out by the new arrivals.

Heather's mum had just managed to get her settled, and Heather had started chatting to the other kids – Jamie, Swifty and Ellie – when a nurse had come and announced that Heather would have to go straight home again. They needed her bed for one of the accident victims.

'Joyriders, aren't they?' she asked, extremely annoyed, as Diane led them out again. After Mags's outburst, word had spread like wildfire. 'Fancy having to make way for thugs!' She caught sight of Diane's worried expression and, unaware that it was caused by other, more personal concerns, said quickly: 'Oh, I'm not blaming you, love! You're just a nurse!'

She disappeared with Heather into the lift, leaving Diane feeling more insignificant than ever on the ward where she'd once been in total charge.

Ellie didn't at all like the disruption to her cosy little world. All the beds had been moved so that the accident victims would be near the office for constant observation. 'Why have they got to change it all?' she murmured to Jamie as another of the teenagers' trolleys was wheeled in. 'And now I've had to miss my X-ray.' She held her stomach. Her pain was starting again . . .

A nurse pulled back the curtains from the two adjacent beds where Sarah and Dan lay propped up, battered and bandaged.

Sarah stared straight ahead, not looking at Dan.

Across the way, two beds still had their curtains closed . . .

'Sarah,' Dan hissed at her side.

She said quietly, still staring straight ahead: 'I told you to slow down.'

He whispered furiously: 'Shut it. Remember, we don't have to tell them anything. Keep your mouth shut.'

Now she did turn, painfully, to look at him. Like her, he was wearing a sling, and there were bruises on his face. He looked as if he was in pain, but he was still belligerent.

She said with quiet horror, 'What about those two girls? Did we kill them?'

'Nah!'

It was just bravado. She turned away again in despair.

Phil's voice came from across the aisle. 'Dan! Sarah! You OK? I've just got bruising.'

'Bust me ribs,' called Dan. 'And done stuff to me neck and arm.' He was wincing. It hurt his chest to speak out loud.

Sarah told Phil: 'Dislocated shoulder, me. They had to push it back, you should have heard me. And I've got a sprained ankle.'

'Seen Jude?' Dan asked Phil.

Phil looked a bit puzzled. 'I heard one of the nurses saying he was in . . . ICU . . . or something. What's that?'

Sarah's heart sank. 'Intensive Care Unit,' she told him. She knew it was bad.

'Oh, he'll be all right,' said Dan, still full of bravado. 'Jude's always all right.'

At that moment the curtains were swished aside from the two beds across the way. Dan looked up instinctively . . . and found himself staring straight into a face: a face already imprinted on his mind. The face in the windscreen as he drove towards it, out of control.

Debbie was staring straight back at him. She screamed. She went on screaming. Beside her, Tanya yelled: 'That's them! They tried to kill us!'

'Shut up!' Dan yelled back, in spite of his pain, 'Shut up!' over and over, while Tanya was bawling: 'They should be in jail, they drove straight at us!' and Debbie went on screaming wordlessly, and all three were yelling as the staff rushed across to calm them.

Once they'd quietened down, the ward was silent. Hostile stares were directed at Dan and Sarah from all along the ward.

'She's lying,' said Dan desperately, but without conviction. 'They were in the way when they shouldn't have been.' His voice faded. No one believed him.

It was clear that it would be necessary to rearrange the ward again. Tanya and Debbie were moved as far from the joyriders as was practicably possible, bearing in mind that all five needed careful observation. Their curtains were drawn across, blocking their view of the kids who'd run them down.

Debbie had finally regained consciousness in Casualty. She had two broken vertebrae, and a very black eye from a bump on her head. They had put her on a drip, and would have to keep a careful eye on her. Above her surgical collar, her face was pale and badly cut.

Tanya had come off more lightly: she had never lost consciousness, and she had been able to complain loudly about the pain in her grazed body and her broken leg.

Along the ward, Sarah lay back, shaken but relieved. So the two girls were not dead.

Dan had gone quiet, and so too had Phil; and Sarah lay trying to squash from her mind the sickening images of the crash.

After some time, she saw Nurse Gallagher go to take Phil's blood pressure. This time he didn't protest. Listlessly, he let her take his arm. When she spoke to him, he only muttered. Nurse Gallagher bent and peered at him. Suddenly she called Sister Mitchell. 'Systolic's only ninety!'

Sister Mitchell was on alert straight away. 'Rob, fetch Kieran!' Then: 'Diane, get a haemacell drip ready.'

Dr Gallagher was on the spot in no time. He pulled the sheets off Phil's abdomen.

'Leave me alone,' Phil protested weakly.

Dan called across: 'Tell them to stuff it, Phil!'

There was no response from Phil.

Kieran pronounced: 'Muscles are rigid. It's the spleen. Ring the surgeon.' And Sister Mitchell was off.

In moments, they'd set up drips, and porters had arrived.

'Phil!' Dan called as they wheeled him past.

Phil's eyes were now closed.

'He's all right,' Sarah protested, trying desperately to convince herself. 'He's just bruised, he said so.' She looked up at Keely, pleading. 'He walked into the ambulance, I saw him.'

Quiet Ellie crept through the curtains to Tanya and Debbie. She told them: 'They just took one of them away. The youngest one. He looked really ill.'

Debbie was still shaken by the sudden confrontation with Dan. Her pale, bruised face set hard. 'Good,' she said. 'I hope he dies.'

In the bleak Intensive Care room, Jude lay unconscious. Impersonal monitors flickered round his bed. Beside him sat his numbed parents.

'Why doesn't he wake up?' Mrs Latimer asked the doctor plaintively.

As Faye had commented to Dr Gallagher, he seemed to be unmarked. His face was swollen but, apart from that and the tube snaking from his nostrils, he could simply be asleep . . .

'We don't really know yet. He's had a full body scan, but even that doesn't give all the answers. It might take us a day or two before we know the extent of the damage.'

'Damage?' she asked faintly, in horror.

'Well, we don't know yet.'

'It's his own fault.' Mr Latimer's voice was choked.

'Alan, don't,' Mrs Latimer begged.

Mr Latimer gazed helplessly at his son. 'We told you this would happen,' he scolded him, as if he were awake, as if he'd just come home as usual, unrepentant and grinning. 'Three times we've had the police round. And did you listen? And look at you now. You stupid little boy.'

He broke down. He picked up Jude's hand. He sobbed: 'Such a little boy.'

Diane thought miserably: it must seem ridiculous, in the face of such tragedy, to be fretting about not getting to the childminder in time. She should have collected Dominic ten minutes ago.

Nervously, she pushed the office door inwards. 'Sandra –'

Sandra Mitchell looked up. 'Have you heard? On

top of everything else, the laundry's out of action! And Lord knows where the pharmaceutical supplies have gone – can you chase them up for me?'

Diane took a deep breath. 'Remember – I asked if I could leave early. I'm really late already . . .'

Sandra looked at her in surprise. 'Yes, but that was before all hell broke loose.'

Diane was going hot. People without children just had no idea . . . She had a vision of the child-minder getting impatient and Dominic sensing it and growing distressed, crying for Diane . . . 'I can't leave Dominic stranded. And Kieran's going to be here till midnight. I'm sorry, Sandra . . .'

Sandra looked at her watch, cool and assessing. 'Well, we can't cover for you. We'll be short till the next shift comes on . . .'

She looked up, resigning herself professionally to a regrettable situation. 'If you must.'

'Sorry . . .' And Diane left, relieved but wretched, feeling messy and selfish and unprofessional. It wasn't fair, she told herself miserably and furiously as she rushed to her car. Babies have to be born. People shouldn't be made to feel like this, just because they have them. But it didn't make her feel any less ridiculous or in the wrong.

As Diane departed, Sister Mitchell's telephone rang.

She listened gravely to the message. When it

ended, she went into the corridor and beckoned Keely.

Neither she nor Keely noticed Faye push her way nervously through the fire doors near by.

'Keely, did you meet Philip Murphy's parents when they first arrived?'

'Yes.'

'Would you mind going back down and giving Kieran a hand?'

'Why, what's up?'

They talked intently, unaware that Faye was standing listening in horror.

'Sarah?' There was a pleading note in Dan's voice now.

Sarah turned to look at Dan at last.

'What's up?' he went on plaintively. 'It's bad enough with all the rest glaring at me!'

She said quietly: 'What's going to happen? That kid with the bandaged hand said the police are hanging around. What'll they do to us?'

He frowned, uncertain. 'Dunno. Jude would know.'

They raised their heads.

Faye was standing by their beds. She looked shocked. She said: 'Phil's dead.'

They stared at her.

'I heard the nurses talking.'

Dan spoke first. 'You've got it wrong!'

Sarah said desperately: 'He walked into the ambulance!'

Sister Mitchell was approaching.

'You're in charge,' Dan shouted at her. 'Tell her! Phil's fine, isn't he?'

Sister Mitchell shook her head. 'I'm sorry. He'd ruptured his spleen and he lost too much blood.'

Dan dropped back on his pillow.

In the next bed, Sarah was saying, over and over, 'But he walked into the ambulance ... He walked ...'

Two

Motherly Mags was devastated.

'I told him he was lucky to be alive!' She was near to tears as she and Student Nurse Keely Johnson crossed the foyer into work next morning. 'And you *told* me to be quiet, didn't you?' She shook her head in despair. 'I must have been one of the last people who spoke to him . . .'

Just ahead of them, in the lift, Sister Sandra Mitchell took a deep breath. The situation on the ward was primed for explosion. She had tried to get either the joyriders or the pedestrians moved to St Mary's, but there had been no spare beds. B1 was stuck with them all on one ward together. It was going to take a lot of hard work to create a calm atmosphere. A lot of tact. And determination on the part of the staff to treat everyone equally, as patients, and not take sides.

She stepped out of the lift and glanced towards the main ward. Then she looked again, unable to believe her eyes. Ladders were leaning on the wall just in front of the door; two young men in overalls were stacking paint tins and whistling in tune to a radio that was playing full blast. That was all they needed, on a ward where tensions were already sky-high.

She went straight to phone the administrator.

She listened in growing cold fury to the administrator's response. 'Yes,' she agreed icily. 'I'll put my complaint in writing. When I get the *time*.'

She put the phone down and sighed angrily. Looked like they were stuck with the decorators too.

There was a knock at the door. Two police officers, one male and one female, were there to interview Sarah and Dan.

From their beds on the ward, Sarah and Dan had seen them arrive.

Tanya's curtains were drawn back, and she saw them as well. 'They've come to get you,' she taunted down the ward.

In view of the situation, Sandra Mitchell and Kieran Gallagher explained to the police, they didn't want Sarah and Dan interviewed on the ward. Kieran would show the police to the interview room to which the two patients would be brought in turn. It was felt that Kieran should be present: the two were still in a state of shock, and Phil's death had made things a whole lot worse.

'And what about the other boy?' the officer asked. 'Jude Latimer?'

'Still in Intensive Care. It doesn't look too good, to be honest.'

Student Nurse Rob brought a wheelchair to take Dan to his police interview.

Dan growled, 'If I'm gonna give a statement, I'll walk.'

'No arguments,' Rob insisted patiently and Dan was forced to give in, scowling.

Student Nurse Keely sat with Sarah, who stared at the bedcover in miserable dread.

The tall young decorator came jauntily past, carrying a stepladder towards the Day Room. He caught sight of them, and of Sarah's face. 'Cheer up, love,' he grinned. 'Might never happen.'

Sandra was right, the decorators could only cause trouble.

Diane approached, bringing Sarah's parents, Mr and Mrs Kulmari, and Keely took the opportunity to pursue the decorator.

She caught up with him in the Day Room. 'Can I have a word with you?'

'Sure.' He introduced himself chirpily. 'Martin.'

She ignored his proffered hand. 'Please be careful what you say on this ward. For many of these kids it *has* happened.'

'Sorry.' He smiled disarmingly. The way he was

looking at her, with interest and appreciation, was making her blush. 'Yes, well,' she said gruffly, turning and going out through the door. 'You can't leave your things in here.'

Something which had been happening recently to Sarah, and which she'd been trying to forget as much as possible, was that her parents were drifting apart. Nowadays it wasn't usual to see them together. It was no comfort, though, to see them together today. They were devastated by what she'd done – the first thing they'd agreed on in months. And now her father came down hard on her. How could she be so *stupid*? What on earth had she been thinking of? And then they began to wrangle, as usual.

'Leave her alone!' her mother told her father. 'She's already under pressure, she's about to see the police.'

'What will they ask me?' Sarah asked anxiously.

'They'll want some straight answers!' her father declared.

Now her mother was at her. 'I don't understand it. How could you get mixed up with that lot? It's not as if we were short of money! You've always had whatever you wanted.'

Sarah hung her head and wished they'd go away again.

*

In the interview room, Dan glared at the table.

'Phil was all right,' he said defensively. 'He could walk. It was *them* that did for him.' He shot an accusing look at Kieran. 'It's neglect, they let him die. They thought: "It's his own fault, he nicked the car, we don't have to look after him, it doesn't matter."'

'And *was* it Phil?' the policeman asked.

There was silence. Dan couldn't do it, put the blame on Phil, little Phil who had just died . . .

The silence went on, and the truth grew and settled in the air of the room. The policeman asked him with calm conviction: 'Why did you steal it, Dan?'

Dan crumpled. He said pathetically: 'It was Jude's idea.'

The interviews were over, and the police had gone.

'They'll want a proper statement after they're discharged,' Sandra told the staff. Her ex-husband was a policeman. 'They're likely to press charges.'

A short while later, Diane was straightening Debbie's bed.

Debbie asked her: 'Can I talk to the police?' She looked troubled.

Diane smiled. 'They've gone now, sweetheart. But you spoke to them yesterday, so there's no need.'

'They should arrest me.'

'Don't be silly,' Diane said gently. 'You've done nothing wrong.'

Debbie frowned as if she just couldn't accept that.

At the entrance to the ward, the decorators were tangling with the new sweet-trolley man, Mr Boswell, rapidly coming to be known as Boz. They had temporarily blocked the way with their ladders, stopping him getting his trolley through to the ward.

He wouldn't wait for them to move. He had a schedule to stick to, he insisted, folding his arms and shaking his bristly head. Those were the rules, and they'd have to move *now*.

Rolling their eyes and deciding that this was a madhouse, they got down off their ladders and made way for him.

He'd not been long on the ward, where staff were thin on the ground, when chaos broke out. Dan called to him from his bed: 'Oy, mister! Chuck us a bar of chocolate!'

From the opposite direction Tanya called to the trolley man: 'Don't give him nothing!'

The man's bristly head swung first right and then left, and then he announced to the air in between and to the ward in general: 'I'm not giving anything to anyone who shouts. Those are the rules: don't let them shout.'

Tanya nevertheless shouted: 'He should starve. He tried to kill us. Drove a car at me and Debbie. He's a murderer. He was in the paper last night, the boy he murdered.'

Boz's eyes bulged as he realized who Dan was. 'I'm not selling to *you*!'

Dan said furiously, 'Who cares what you think? It's your job to sell chocolate, so sell me some chocolate, thicko.'

The man's chest swelled with anger. 'I'm Mr Boswell to you!'

The raised voices reached the staff meeting in the office. Diane rushed out to handle things.

Sarah was urging: 'Dan, just leave it –' but all she got from him was a glare, and from Tanya the loud cry: 'Don't listen to her, she was driving too!'

Boz's eyes bulged further as he surveyed both Dan and Sarah. He announced to them: 'I'm going to administration over this. You should be in a separate place. With bars on the windows.' As Diane swooped towards him, he turned on her: 'You lot aren't doing your job. You'd have me selling to convicted criminals.'

Diane was steely. 'Can I have a word with you, Mr Boswell?'

'I haven't finished my round! I've got to finish, there are rules!'

Tanya called to Diane: 'Leave him alone, he's on our side!'

'Right now,' Diane told him icily, and before he could argue, she had taken hold of his trolley and was marching with it out of the ward.

'Hey,' he called, following, outraged. 'No one but me's allowed to touch that!'

She parked it halfway down the corridor and rounded on him. 'Mr Boswell, I know you're new here, so there's a few things you should learn. You can't stand in the middle of the ward and make accusations. It's not for us to take sides.'

Boz shook his head. Then he squared up to her and wagged a finger. 'Listen, you're a nurse, that's your job, not to have opinions or take sides. It's not mine. I know *my* job, and that's not part of it. If I meet a murderer, I don't have to just smile and carry on.'

And he swept off with his trolley and his strong opinions, which of course he'd be bringing back again next day.

The situation was becoming more of a nightmare with every moment.

'This is just the start,' Sandra warned, back in the office. 'Dealing with the parents will be the worst.'

At that moment, Tom Swift, Swifty's father, put his bushy, cheery head round the office door. 'Ah,

Sandra, I can see you're busy,' he said cheerily, and drew it back out again.

'It's not a good time, Tom,' she smiled ruefully, a few minutes later in the corridor. 'In fact, it couldn't be worse. I'll phone you tonight.'

'Okey-doke,' he grinned amiably. He left her to her work and looked around for Swifty, who'd be bound to be up to mischief somewhere.

Near the lifts the decorators were shifting some equipment. 'Whoops, mind yourself,' Tom Swift said, helpfully clearing a large sign, placed in front of the lifts, out of the way.

It was Swifty, coming in a direction he shouldn't be, with his partner in crime, Jamie, and their surprising new confederate, quiet Ellie. 'Come on, Sean,' said his father, 'before you get into any more mischief.' And he stepped backwards into the open lift – the lift which, a moment before, had been blocked by a sign saying DANGER: OUT OF ORDER – and fell into the shaft.

Fortunately the lift was stuck just below floor level, but Tom had strained his back in the fall.

'I've a good mind to sue them!' he announced in his bed on Male Orthopaedics, looking up at Swifty and Sandra Mitchell, who were sitting, one each side of him.

'I'm sure you could,' said Sandra, 'if you hadn't removed the sign yourself.' She was unable to suppress a little smile. Swifty's accident-proneness was obviously an inherited trait.

'The problem now is you, Sean,' Tom said anxiously. Who would look after him while Tom was in hospital? 'You can't stay with your mother, she's on a course in Scotland.' He paused, then asked nervously: 'Sandra, I don't suppose . . . you could move into the house, just for a few days . . .?'

Swifty was horrified. And Sandra wasn't exactly thrilled either. 'It's not so easy, Tom,' she replied awkwardly. 'I've only been in the new flat a month, and I haven't yet had alarms fitted. I wouldn't like to leave it empty.'

'See?' said Swifty in relief.

Then Sandra dropped a bombshell for Swifty. 'I have got a spare room,' she smiled, realizing that there was no other option. And it was the least she could do for this man who had helped her to recover from the sadness of her divorce. Even if children – especially the bundle of mischief that was Swifty – didn't exactly fit into her neat, orderly life.

Swifty stared at her in dismay. One of his worst fears *was* about to be realized . . .

At five o'clock Sandra was putting on her coat. She told Diane anxiously: 'I'm really sorry to be leaving you in the lurch like this. Only I've got to help Sean pack his things up at home, and move him to my flat, and I'd better get to the supermarket if I'm going to have to feed him.'

'I've done it before – *remember*?' Diane reminded her, not without a little irritation.

But it wasn't that Sandra didn't think Diane would cope. She asked anxiously: 'You won't be late? With the childminder?'

Diane shook her head in reassurance and smiled. How quickly the tables had turned, she thought. How quickly you come to understand the problems, once you're in charge of a child.

Kieran had been examining Dan.

'If you keep on like this, these ribs aren't going to get better,' he told him.

Dan scowled. 'I should ask for another doctor. After how you treated Phil.'

Kieran looked at him seriously. 'Dan, we're doctors, not God. We can't know everything.'

This prompted Sarah in the next bed to ask worriedly: 'Dr Gallagher. What about Jude?'

'They're still doing tests. It might be a while yet before we know exactly what's wrong.'

Panic slid across her face. 'So he hasn't woken up yet?'

Dan was looking away, avoiding their gaze.

'No. But that's not to say that he won't.'

'But if it's brain damage . . .?' She forced herself to ask, dreading the answer. 'Will it be permanent?'

'Sarah, I wish I could give you an answer. The human brain's the most complicated thing in the world. And the most fragile. All that protects it is a single layer of bone. If we'd designed it ourselves, we'd be taken to court for breach of safety regulations. And the skull doesn't even need to break for harm to be done. If your brain gets shaken up, then everything gets shaken up – your thoughts, your instincts, your reflexes, all in a mess. Sometimes we don't even know where to begin mending it.'

Then he smiled. 'But at the same time, the brain's remarkably powerful. It can heal itself in ways that hospitals can only guess at. So you needn't give up hope.'

Sarah said suddenly: 'I want to speak to his mum. It's our fault.'

Dan was furious. 'It's not!' he told Dr Gallagher. 'Jude told us to get the car. Jude gave us instructions . . .'

In Intensive Care, Mr and Mrs Latimer were sitting beside their still unconscious son.

They felt helpless, confused. They found it hard to take in what the doctors were saying. Jude had been given an EEG, an electroencephalogram, in which electrodes had been placed on his scalp to check on the electrical activity in his brain. To see where it might be damaged . . . There *was* activity, but the doctors could not yet say what state Jude would be in for the rest of his life . . .

It was all so unreal, they could hardly believe it was happening. That this lifeless-seeming body could be their grinning wisecracking son . . .

And his sister, Leanne, how could she understand? She had wanted to come and see him, but how could she cope with it? They had had to tell her that he was just asleep, and that they'd bring her in when he woke. In the meantime they'd placed her photo at his side, so that he'd see it when he woke . . .

If he woke . . .

Mrs Latimer stood up and went to get a cup of coffee, to stop herself breaking down.

As she stepped into the corridor, she caught sight of someone she recognized. That girl Jude had been going out with. Faye. She was making for the ward, shaking back her straggly blonde hair as she went. Mrs Latimer didn't like her, but . . .

'Faye!' she called out.

Faye turned. She looked guilty, and unwilling.

'Are you going to visit Jude?'

Faye shrugged. She seemed embarrassed and ashamed. 'Dunno. I *was* going to see Sarah.'

Mrs Latimer hesitated. 'He's still in a coma. But they said he might be able to hear. You could talk to him.'

Faye said, miserable and sullen: 'You didn't like me coming round to your house, though.'

Mrs Latimer bit her lip. 'But does that matter now? They said we should surround him with things he likes – music and things. *You* know what he likes, what bands . . . I don't . . .' And at the thought of that, Mrs Latimer's face began trembling with tears.

Faye looked down, avoiding the sight of her crying. 'Later,' she muttered. 'If I've got time.'

And she turned away and was gone, off into the ward.

The fact was, Faye simply couldn't face it. The thought of Jude, tall, witty Jude, reduced to a brain-damaged body on a slab . . . Someone had said he could end up a vegetable . . . It was almost worse than just dying, like Phil . . .

She shut her mind to it, and plonked herself down beside Sarah.

Dan wasn't there. Sarah nodded to where he could be seen in the Day Room. He had dragged himself there, and now sat, hunched. 'He's been like that ever since,' Sarah told her morosely. 'When his whole life has been dedicated to having a laugh . . .'

The two were silent.

Then Sarah asked her anxiously: 'So how's Jude?'

Faye started with guilt. 'I dunno,' she confessed.

Sarah was aghast. 'Haven't you been to see him?'

She lied quickly. 'They don't want me there, it's family only.'

Sarah was indignant. 'Well, you should insist! You know him better than anyone. And he needs to be near his friends, voices he knows, that Dr Gallagher told me.' She became urgent. 'Don't listen to his mum, you push your way in there. He's your boyfriend, for God's sake!'

'Yeah,' said Faye. 'Yeah, you're right.' Knowing that she was.

Over at Debbie's bed, her elder brother, Tim, was visiting her. Tanya was giggling at his jokes, but there seemed to be no way he could cheer Debbie up. He was worried. Her skull had been X-rayed, and she had a bruised kidney, but they'd said she was OK. Something was definitely wrong, though.

'Come on, Debs,' he said finally. 'Give us a smile.'

'I'm tired,' she said wanly.

'No, she's not,' Tanya pronounced. 'It's *that* lot.' She pointed at Faye and Sarah, and then at Dan, brooding in the Day Room. 'That's him. The boy who was driving.'

So that was it. Dan Miller. Tim stiffened, staring intently at Dan. Then without another word he got up and made his way towards the Day Room.

He stood in front of Dan, menacing. He reached out and grabbed his sling. It was only a light touch, but Dan winced with pain. Tim hissed: 'Shall I hurt you? Like you hurt my nine-year-old sister?'

Dan growled through his pain: 'Sent you, did she? Doing a little girl's work?'

Tim bent towards him. 'Tell me, Dan Miller, how come your friend ends up brain-dead, but he's still smarter than you?'

Dan stood up and flailed at him, but Tim grabbed his painful arm. Tim spat into his face: 'What you gonna do? Call for your mates? One's dead and the other's half there. You're nothing without your pathetic little gang. Nothing.'

'All right, boys, let it go.'

They turned to see Martin, the tall decorator, standing in the doorway.

For some seconds Tim kept hold of Dan, then, as Martin called for a nurse, he shoved him back into his chair. 'I'll see you again,' he told him, then he pushed past Martin, and Keely and Diane, who had come running.

'Thanks,' Keely said gratefully to Martin, as they left Dan to Diane. She'd misjudged Martin: he'd proved an antidote to trouble. She smiled at him warmly, and he gave her a wry, no-problem grin.

Diane looked at Dan. He was crying, and angry at her for seeing it. He burst out at her, shouting: 'I didn't kill him! He was my mate!'

In the ward, they all heard it. His choked voice

betrayed that he was crying. That tough lad, that gang member . . . Even Tanya was silent.

Diane knelt by his chair.

He had quietened. He sobbed: 'He wanted to come with us. I didn't force him. I used to tell him to push off, he was always hanging around. It's not my fault. It's not . . .'

Tears rolled down his sallow cheeks.

And in the main ward, tears rolled down Debbie's, too.

Homely Mags was straightening Debbie's pillow.

'Mags?' Debbie asked nervously. 'Will they let me go home?'

''Course they will! Once you're better.'

Debbie looked up with wide, fearful eyes. 'They won't send me to prison?'

Mags sat down on her bed in concern. 'Of course not! Now, what's put that idea into your head?'

'I said I hope he dies. Phil Murphy. And he did.' She started to cry.

'Oh, love!' Mags gathered her up in a cuddle. 'That's not why he died. Saying something doesn't make it happen.'

Debbie peered at her face anxiously.

'Look,' said Mags, 'if you wished for a million ice-creams, they wouldn't just appear, would they?'

'No . . .'

'Well then.'

And Mags felt Debbie relax as she became reassured.

Mags squeezed her. 'We all say things we don't mean. Even grown-ups like me, when we're angry or upset.'

Poor Mags was near to tears, too, thinking of her own words to Phil just before he died.

Faye crept nervously in through the Intensive Care room door.

Mrs Latimer was there, bending wearily over the bed. She looked up.

'I'm not staying,' Faye muttered.

'That's all right.' Mrs Latimer stood and gave her her chair. 'Every little helps. Shall I leave you on your own?'

Faye shrugged. 'If you want.'

Mrs Latimer hesitated and then left, and Faye was relieved – though the next moment she was horrified at being left there with Jude, alone except for the nurse.

She forced herself to look. The machines flickered. There were tubes everywhere. But it *was* still Jude: face expressionless, eyes closed, but his long, handsome features still the same.

The nurse was beside her. 'Talk to him,' she suggested.

Faye felt stupid. 'What shall I say?'

'Anything.' And the nurse went back to her desk.

Faye looked at Jude's sallow, sheeny face again. She cleared her throat. With difficulty she said: 'Someone nicked Morrie's bike.' Jude's face was immobile, but she went on: 'He said he wished you were there, you'd find out who did it.' And then she got into the swing of it, and told him how it had happened.

But there was no response. Not a flicker. After a while she ran out of things to say.

She couldn't stand it any more. It was too spooky, too scary. She thought: if he could hear through that lot, then maybe he could even read her mind.

'I'd better get off,' she said awkwardly.

He opened his eyes and shut them.

Her heart turned over. 'Nurse!' she cried. 'He opened his eyes!'

The nurse came running over. 'Step back, Faye, let me look.' She bent over him. 'Jude? Hello?'

Jude opened his eyes wide.

Faye cried: 'He's gonna be all right, isn't he? I knew he would be!'

But the nurse was saying, 'Jude? Hello? Can you hear me?' And there was not a flicker of response, no awareness in Jude's wide, unseeing eyes.

Three

In the ward kitchen Keely quoted by heart from the nursing textbook:

'If the brain is displaced, the only escape valve is the tentorial hiatus, and the third cranial nerve ceases to function.'

Rob was testing her as she loaded up the breakfast trolley. Their exams were tomorrow.

'Swot!' he said in rueful admiration. He wasn't at all confident himself.

She finished the trolley and he put the book down and together they wheeled the breakfast through to the ward. In the corridor, Kieran Gallagher shuffled aside for them and, knowing how they were feeling, gave them an ironic thumbs-up.

Kieran popped his head into the office, where Diane had now arrived. 'Dominic settle all right at the childminder's?' he asked.

She nodded. 'I hate leaving him, though.' And she'd only just got here on time.

'Sandra not here yet?'

She shook her head, sharing his surprise.

Kieran couldn't wait, he was in a hurry. 'Well, Jude Latimer's ready to come up from ICU. He's still not responding, but he's off the ventilator, and the stimulation he'll get here could help.'

She nodded. 'Sally Watson's gone home, so we can make space.'

As he turned back to the door, Sandra Mitchell arrived. She looked strangely rushed and a little dishevelled, and they remembered: Swifty! 'Had a nice peaceful breakfast?' Kieran asked her.

She groaned. 'He insisted on making it! And I thought: well, you can't discourage it, can you, if they show any inclination to take responsibility? But you should have seen the *mess*! So that's why I'm a bit late . . .' She looked round guiltily.

Kieran grinned and ducked away.

Diane told her: 'Jude Latimer's ready to come on to the ward. I said we'd make space.'

Sandra was put out. 'First I've heard of it,' she said coldly. 'So much for consultation.' Only two minutes late, and they'd taken over in her absence, turned themselves into a husband-and-wife team. She had a panicky feeling that life with Sean was going to mean life out of control . . .

Martin the decorator caught the edge of Sandra's ruffled temper. As she stepped into the corridor, he commented cheerily: 'I bet that Florence Nightingale was a student nurse when this last had a lick of paint.'

She retorted sharply: 'And I'll have retired by the time you've finished this one.' Then she proceeded to deliver him a warning about lack of attention to safety procedures.

Sarah and Dan watched solemnly as the nurses and doctors wheeled Jude's bed on to the ward. His still body, the oxygen mask, the tubes snaking under the covers from various plastic bags . . .

Sarah looked away. She whispered: 'If we hadn't done it . . . none of this would have happened.' She turned in anguish to Dan. '*Why* did you always jump when Jude clicked his fingers?'

He was white and hunched. He'd been even more subdued since the tussle with Debbie's brother yesterday. 'We all did. All of us. Phil . . .'

'Phil's *dead*!'

Dan was silent. Across the way, they were settling Jude's drip-stand and hooking up his catheter bag. Then they pulled the curtains round him and Jude was hidden from view.

Dan said in a low voice: 'We should go.'

'Go where?'

'To the funeral.'

To the funeral . . . She thought about it. It would be weird, she'd never been to a funeral. But it would make it somehow not so bad, like telling Phil what they felt, telling him how hard they wished it hadn't happened . . . And they knew where the funeral was and what time, at half-past twelve, later this morning – that auxiliary, Mags, had been telling Nurse Keely she was going, and now that Sarah had a wheelchair, Dan could push her.

She opened her mouth to say these things to Dan, and her eyes met those of Debbie's brother coming into the ward again. He glared back at her. 'What's it like going out with a murderer?'

'Butt out, scuz!' she spat, though her voice was choked.

Tim let his contemptuous gaze drop on Dan. 'Letting your girlfriend do your fighting? Weedy get.'

'Bog off,' Dan bawled, and Sarah yelled, her voice high with her emotions: 'Trying to impress your little fan club?'

Right on cue, Tanya chimed in: 'You nearly killed my best friend!'

Diane was down on them. '*What's* going on?'

'You should have left them in the road,' Tim yelled at her.

'They don't deserve treatment!' Tanya called.

'You should ban him!' came from Dan.

Diane restored order with difficulty and led Tim away up the ward. She told him quietly: 'We can't have World War Three breaking out every time you appear.'

He was still wound up. 'It cracks me up, seeing them two! Our Debs could have died.'

But at last she calmed him down. 'Sorry,' he muttered, and went off past them to see Debbie without any further aggro.

Diane sighed with relief. Too soon. As he reached Debbie's bed, Tanya's voice rang out: 'Are you going to get them, Tim?'

Kieran came in, on his way to examine Jude. Sarah asked him: 'Dr Gallagher, we can go to Phil's funeral, can't we?'

Kieran shook his head. 'I'm sorry. Neither of you is fit enough.'

Then they all caught sight of Faye, hovering in the ward entrance and looking uncertainly at the curtains round Jude.

Kieran told her: 'You should be able to see him soon,' and then he disappeared inside the curtains.

Faye looked horrified. She turned in relief to Sarah and Dan.

Sarah told her: 'They won't let us go to Phil's funeral.'

Dan added: 'He's a waste of space, Gallagher.'

'What d'you expect?' said Faye, hard again. 'They're as bad as teachers, this lot. What d'you want to go for, though?' She looked at them as if they were mad.

Dan looked away. Sarah mumbled, 'Dunno . . . Say goodbye, like.'

Faye snorted. 'What's the point? You've got to get on with life.'

'But we can't just forget him!'

'You don't have to. But what's the point being morbid? He was a right laugh, Phil. I wouldn't go. But if I wanted to, I wouldn't let *them* stop me.'

She looked less sure of herself as the staff began to emerge from the curtains opposite. 'Make sure he's as comfortable as possible,' Dr Gallagher was telling Rob, 'because he can't tell us when he's not.'

He beckoned to her. 'You can see him now, Faye.'

She forced herself to go over to where Jude was lying, propped against the pillows. Those staring, blinking, empty eyes . . . She wanted to look away again.

'We don't know if he can see,' Dr Gallagher told her.

As if they needed to tell her. She asked roughly: 'Can he hear?'

'We don't know. But he's alive. And he needs all the care and attention possible –'

She broke in: 'What's the point of being here? What can *I* do?'

And she stared at Jude almost as if she hated him.

Because their beds were near the entrance, it was fairly easy to slip out. Dan hobbled, pushing the wheelchair one-handed, and without hindrance they were into the lift and away.

They had reached the cemetery before the staff on the ward realized they'd gone.

Wearily, painfully, Dan brought the wheelchair to a halt. Fifty yards off, the mourners were gathered round the grave. Men and women in black, and schoolchildren in naff posh uniforms. Sarah was overcome by the horror of it: like her, Phil had led a completely double life . . . She thought of his mother. The droning voice of the vicar came towards them, and the sound of sobs . . . She said: 'Hold on, I'm scared.'

But Dan was already pushing forward again, and they were drawing near the group of mourners –

The vicar intoned: 'We have entrusted Philip to God's merciful keeping, and we now commit him to the ground.'

Between the legs, Sarah could make out the rectangular gash in the ground. A gaping hole for little Philip's body . . .

Mrs Murphy looked up and saw them.

Bulbous with tears, monstrous with grief, Mrs Murphy screamed: 'Get away! You shouldn't be here! You killed him! Get away!'

She lunged at the wheelchair and tried to push it away; she gasped, she slobbered, she seemed about to faint; people caught her and held her, bent at the knees.

Dan and Sarah were frozen with horror.

Mags rushed forward, her own face bruised and swollen by tears. She grabbed the wheelchair and turned it about, but not before Sarah had seen the ranks of stony faces ranged in hatred against her and Dan.

She was shaking as Mags wheeled her back to the hospital, Dan trailing painfully behind.

On the ward, they were searching everywhere.

Tanya tried to tell them: 'They've done a bunk, I saw them!' but they'd long since stopped listening to what she called out about Sarah and Dan.

Faye could have told them, but they assumed that she was far too preoccupied with Jude to know.

As she sat beside him miserably, his parents arrived.

She stood quickly, relieved at this chance of escape, but Mrs Latimer said: 'You don't have to go, Faye.'

Mrs Latimer didn't actually look as though she really meant it, and Faye hung about awkwardly, not knowing what to do.

Mrs Latimer glanced at her vacantly staring son and asked Faye: 'How is he?'

What a stupid question, it didn't deserve an answer. Faye shrugged sullenly.

She saw Mrs Latimer's lips tighten in anger.

Mr Latimer took out a picture which Jude's kid

sister had obviously drawn. 'This is for you, Jude,' he told the mask-like face.

Faye felt ill. It was all so hideous, so pathetic. She said harshly: 'He can't see it!'

There was a hot silence, and then Mrs Latimer turned on her: 'Why did you let him get mixed up in all this?' She was trembling and her snooty-woman's cheekbones were shiny and red.

'Me?'

'He'd have listened to you! You saw more of him!' And now the stupid woman was blubbering. 'It's destroyed his dad.'

'Hah! It's a great laugh for me!' A coil of fury unwound inside Faye.

Mr Latimer tried to calm them. 'I know you're upset,' he told Faye.

She snarled contemptuously: 'You don't know *anything* about me!'

Mrs Latimer cried: 'I know *you* got off scot free.' Her lips were curled in distaste. 'Don't say you've never been in a stolen car. I've seen you girls, egging them on!'

Faye felt wild. 'I'm not to blame – it's *you*! The reason you never saw Jude was he couldn't stand being in the house! You never bothered what he was up to! Well, it's a bit late now!'

Mrs Latimer exploded. 'I know your type! You're nothing but a slag! Jude could do better. And he knew that, he was going to chuck you!'

'Liar!' Faye felt as though someone had punched her in the chest. Chuck her? Well, he had, hadn't he? He'd just gone, leaving nothing behind but this lifeless, no-good, dribbling body.

She turned on her heel and left.

She came back when she thought Sarah and Dan would be back as well. They were: they'd been well bawled out by Sister Mitchell.

'And Mrs Murphy went bananas,' Dan told her,

'Well,' said Sarah, 'she was upset!' She was still upset herself.

Sarah was being a real wimp, Faye thought. She could see that Dan thought so too.

'I don't know why you bothered going,' she told them. 'You only get grief from any of 'em, even when you try and do the right thing.' She glared across at the Latimers.

'Gallagher's all right,' said Sarah. He'd not got at them about the funeral, the way bat-face Sister Mitchell had.

Faye sneered. 'He gets right up my nose. Trying to be all pally. Telling me what's best for Jude.'

She nodded towards the Latimers. 'Look at them, may as well talk to a brick wall.'

Just then, though, the Latimers stood up and got themselves together and left.

Sarah and Dan were looking at Faye expectantly,

waiting for her to take over at Jude's side. To do her duty, as his girlfriend.

Faye stood up. 'OK,' she said finally, almost sarcastically. 'I'm going to see my *boyfriend*.'

She stepped out towards Jude's bed. To her horror, at that moment Rob came through the doors towards her, carrying something covered on a tray. 'I'll just see to him, Faye, before you settle,' he said, beginning to draw the curtain across her way.

See to him? She saw what was on the tray. She was horrified, she felt like gagging.

'Change his *nappy*, you mean!' she said savagely, and ran from the ward.

In the corridor she collapsed against the wall. She couldn't bear it, everyone expecting her to feel what she couldn't, when she felt just the opposite . . .

She looked up. Dan had hobbled after her.

'Have you seen the state of him?' she cried.

'Don't listen to that lot. Jude's got more bottle than any of them. He'll be all right.'

'He can't do anything for himself – eat, talk, go to the bog. Like a baby!'

'They can just come round, I've seen it on telly.'

'It's a con. He might as well be dead.' And to Dan's surprise she burst out crying and flung herself against him, burying her face in his shoulder and clinging on.

Experimentally, he put his good arm on her back.

She nuzzled in further.

He looked up. Sarah was standing some feet away, watching it all.

Four

At midday the next day, a tough-looking lad of about fifteen parked his bike at the entrance to a neat maisonette, two miles from South Park Hospital. He made his way up the stairs to the first-floor flat whose windows were protected by wrought-iron bars. Five minutes later he emerged with a padded envelope tucked inside his jacket. He mounted his bike and set off. Not long afterwards he turned off down a narrow side road that led over the canal, towards his destination for delivery.

As he made the brow of the hump-backed bridge, he heard the engine of a motorbike tearing along towards the corner behind him. He stood on his pedals. If he didn't make it off the bridge quickly, the vehicle would be on him. The motorcycle scoured round the bend and up the bridge. On the other side, the pedal-cyclist suddenly came into the rider's view, right ahead; he tried to swerve; he hit the pushbike a glancing blow, and the lad hurtled through the air and over the parapet of the bridge, the packet going flying.

The motorcyclist came to a halt, his heart thudding. He felt sick.

He dismounted. The lad sat up, dazed.

'You all right, son?'

The youth winced in pain. His face was white.

'I'll go and get help.' The motorcyclist hesitated a moment or two longer, uncertain whether the boy should be left alone. Then, seeing no other option, he got back on his bike and drove off to find a phone box.

The lad saw where the package was lying, half hidden in the bushes. He tried to get up, but collapsed back, gasping with pain. When the pain had subsided, he dragged himself across the ground and retrieved it. He began to push it back inside his jacket, and then stopped. The biker would be ringing for an ambulance. He pushed it back under the bushes. With difficulty, in severe pain, he jammed it under some stones against the wall.

He lay back and passed out.

Kieran was called off the ward to see him in Casualty.

'I see Jude's not had his NG tube in yet,' he commented to Sandra Mitchell on his way out.

She prickled. 'We're short-staffed. Keely and Rob

are sitting their exams this morning. We're doing our best.'

She saw with irritation that someone wasn't. Martin the decorator was standing at Debbie's bed chatting to her and Tanya.

They were staring at him, half in disbelief, half in admiration. 'What?' cried Tanya. 'You *really* were nearly in Take That?' She peered up at his grinning face, uncertain whether he was joking. She wanted to believe him. 'Well, why weren't you, then?' she demanded, challenging him.

He grinned wickedly. 'I'm telling you. Jealousy. Too good-looking.'

'Well, you didn't write any of their songs!'

'Yeah, I did. "Babe". Thought that one up in the bath. Dead easy.'

'Wow. Well, that's dead rotten, not giving you credit!'

Martin was let off the hook by Sister Mitchell's sharp reminder: 'Haven't you got work to do?'

'Just getting my spirit level,' he grinned, and scooted.

Sarah was utterly miserable. This morning her mother had been in, and had told her that the neighbours were beginning to talk, about the crash and about it all being in the papers. And about what had happened at the funeral.

'You do some silly things at times,' her mother

had said about the funeral. As if Sarah didn't feel bad enough about it already. And it *wasn't* silly, why should it be? Phil had been their friend; it was *right,* not silly, for them to be there. But no allowance was made for that, no allowance for *their* feelings, not now, not after what they'd done. Or ever.

Her mother started going on about her father: it had been *his* turn to come, and yet he hadn't turned up: how did she think Sarah felt about *that*? That was all they thought of her: not a person with her own feelings, but a burden they had to take turns over. She had wanted to cry.

And now Faye had turned up. Sarah and Dan had said nothing to each other about what had happened the night before, but, the minute Faye arrived, Dan followed her to the Day Room. Sarah hobbled after them on the walking-stick she'd now been given, feeling uninvited.

Faye had brought a bottle of orange juice, doctored with vodka. She flopped down on the seat next to Dan and lolled on him ostentatiously as she handed him the bottle. Now it was Faye and Dan who didn't care about Sarah's feelings. Worse: Faye seemed to be deliberately making Sarah feel bad.

Dan took a good swig. 'This ward's dead,' he said. 'I can't wait to get out.'

'Yeah,' said Faye, leaning on him. 'We'll have a right laugh.'

'I'll show you what a good driver I am. No messing *this* time.' He pointed accusingly at Sarah, the one who'd been chicken, who'd kept saying *Slow down*.

Sarah cried in disbelief: 'What, nick another car? After what's happened –'

Faye cut her off. 'Hey, Dan,' she said, ignoring Sarah in an exaggerated way. 'Remember that time you were bombing down Parkway and did a U-turn across the reservation?'

'When?' Sarah cried. She knew nothing about this.

Faye gave a nasty laugh. Dan was grinning at the memory: 'Smart or what?'

What had been going on? Looked liked Faye had begun to get her hooks in well before now.

The Day Room door burst open. Tanya stood there on her new crutches, eyes shining with fury, with Ellie right behind. 'Right, who's had him?'

The teenagers turned and stared at her. 'Who?' Faye asked, as though she were about to swat a fly.

'Tony.'

What was the squirt on about? This was the last thing Sarah wanted to be bothered with right now. 'Get lost!' she told her.

'Give it back,' Tanya demanded. 'Give me back Tony, my troll.'

Dan and Faye burst out laughing derisively.

'We've not had your stupid troll,' said Sarah, irritable and savage.

Tanya stepped up to her. 'Give it me, you *murderer!*'

That was it. Sarah snapped. She stood. 'Get out of my face.' And she pushed her. For one horrible moment, Tanya toppled with her crutches, but then she managed to right herself. She turned away, followed by Ellie, defeated for now, but intent on revenge.

'Ooooh!' Faye called mockingly, at Sarah's temper.

Sarah grabbed the bottle off Dan and took a big swig.

When she took it away from her mouth again, she saw them exchanging 'get her' looks.

The injured fifteen-year-old cyclist was brought up to the ward.

He was still drifting in and out of consciousness.

'Hello?' Kieran said to him, as he came to once more. 'You've had an accident. You're at South Park Hospital.'

The boy put his hand instinctively to his chest, as if looking for something, but then he seemed to remember, and he closed his eyes in relief.

'What's your full name?' Kieran asked him once more. 'Are you on the phone at home?'

'Simmo . . . Paul Simmondson . . .' The lad's eyes

suddenly jerked wide open. 'When can I get out of here?' he asked.

'You won't be moving anywhere for a few days. You've had a nasty bump on your head and you've fractured your ankle.'

Simmo gave a groan and drifted off again.

At last he regained full consciousness, and about fifteen minutes later Diane Gallagher noticed a couple sitting by his bed. They must be his parents, Mr and Mrs Simmondson. There was something about them, she thought . . . The woman was very flashy, and the man looked something of a thug . . . Still, they must be good parents to have turned up so promptly, and Diane pulled herself up for making snobbish judgements.

She would have trusted her first instincts if she could have heard what was being said at Simmo's bed.

'How did you know I was in here?' Simmo asked them sullenly.

The woman, Cath, smiled at him brightly, but her eyes were hard. 'I make it my business to know things.'

The man, Bernard, said nothing.

'So where is it?'

Simmo glowered at her resentfully. That was all she was worried about. Not the slightest care about what had happened to him. 'Someone must have lifted it. When I was out cold in the road. That bloke who hit me, maybe . . .'

But she put her hand on his injured leg and squeezed. He gasped in pain.

Behind her, Bernard folded his arms threateningly.

She leaned forward, into Simmo's face. Diane, glancing up from across the ward, thought she was kissing him. Cath hissed, 'I want that package.'

And when Diane looked up again, intending to catch her for Simmo's details, she and the man had gone.

As the man and woman went out through the hospital gates, a ten-year-old girl was making her own way in, nervous but determined. In her hand she clasped the painting she'd most recently done for her brother. She would give it to Jude herself. They hadn't kept their word. They had said that when he woke up she could go and see him; now they said he had, but they were still refusing to take her. They said he wasn't well enough. But she could help to make him better . . .

She gazed up at the clustered signs, and stood looking from right to left, confused. She spotted the sign for Children's Ward and headed off in that direction.

She climbed the stairs and saw the sign which told her to turn left. She set out along the corridor.

There was the entrance: CHILDREN'S WARD B1. She turned in. Through the doors she could see bright curtains, and the heads of children darting about. She pushed on the door.

Mr and Mrs Latimer saw Leanne standing there before she saw them. Mr Latimer quickly pulled the curtains across Jude's bed. By the time she caught sight of them, he was hidden and her parents had moved away from him.

'Leanne!' they cried, rushing to her side. 'What are you doing here?'

'I want to see Jude!' Her eyes scanned the ward behind them, looking for him.

They led her out quickly. She craned back, searching, and complained: 'You come to see him all the time! Why have *I* got to wait?' Now she was suspicious. 'Jude *is* getting better, isn't he?' she asked them solemnly in the waiting room.

'Of course! Of course!' They couldn't bear to confront her with the truth, even now that she had demanded it.

'So can I see him then?' she challenged, and stood up.

Mrs Latimer lied wildly: 'He's just gone down to physiotherapy.'

'I'll wait then.' There was a look of calm stubbornness on her face.

Mr Latimer said, panicky: 'He'll need to sleep when he gets back.'

She moved to the door. 'I want to see him. Where is he?'

Her mother stood in her way. 'Not here, I told you. Look, we'll leave your picture with the nurses. We can all go home together.'

And the Latimers led her away, homewards. She was puzzled. They'd seemed to be lying, but they couldn't have been. They'd have gone to say good-bye if Jude had been on the ward . . .

So far as Dan and Faye were concerned, it seemed, Jude hardly existed any more. For a short while they all sat round his bed, but Dan and Faye talked across him, ignoring him as he gazed vacantly past them, remembering good times with the gang and looking forward to future ones.

'You fancy her, don't you?' Sarah dared to challenge Dan finally, when Faye went to the toilets.

It wasn't a straight answer, but it told her enough. 'You've really got on my nerves since we landed here. All you do is moan and feel sorry for yourself.'

'But how can you two talk as if nothing has happened?'

'I expect sermons from them out there – but from *you*?!'

She asked miserably: 'Do you want to finish with me?'

He didn't answer.

At that moment Faye came back in. 'What's up?' she asked blithely, insolently, and flopped down close to Dan. 'Cheers!' she cried as he handed her the bottle.

Tim was visiting Debbie and they were playing Scrabble with Tanya.

Debbie and Tanya had plenty of news to tell.

Nurse Gallagher had said that Debbie would probably be able to get up out of bed soon.

Then there was the business of the troll going missing. It hadn't been found. And, not long afterwards, the Travel Scrabble which Tim had brought in for Debbie had gone missing too – which was why they were now having to play with the Day Room set. Debbie and Tanya and Ellie were sure there was a thief about. Ellie had thought of a plot to catch the culprit. They'd smeared the underside of Debbie's Take That album with some grease the painters had left lying around. Anyone nicking it would get grease all over, and be well and truly marked.

'Your Take That album?' Tim said, amazed. 'Won't it ruin it?'

'Yeah,' said Debbie airily. 'I don't care, they deserve it. After what they did to Martin, nicking his song.'

'It'll be one of *them* thieving,' Tanya said darkly, nodding towards the gang in the Day Room. And here was the most important thing Tanya had to tell him: '*She* threatened me.' She pointed out Sarah. 'Tried to knock me over.'

Tim looked grim.

Not long afterwards, the Day Room door opened and Sarah came out. Tim stiffened.

Sarah looked across at them and hesitated. Then she seemed to make a decision, and hopped across.

Surprisingly, she seemed embarrassed. She said to Tanya: 'I wanted to say sorry. About before.' She turned to Tim. 'And I'm sorry for mouthing off at you.' She shrugged awkwardly and gestured vaguely at the ward. 'This place gets to you.'

For a moment, as she hung there, no one answered.

Then Tim said, just as awkwardly, 'Yeah . . . Yeah, it must.'

There was another silence, and then, to everyone's surprise, Sarah sat down. 'Who's winning?'

When Faye and Dan came out of the Day Room a few minutes later, they couldn't have been more surprised or disgusted at the sight which met their eyes: Sarah sitting playing Scrabble with that lot, laughing and engrossed.

Well, that settled it, didn't it?

Sandra Mitchell was weary.

As if she hadn't got enough on her plate, here was Tom shuffling up from Male Orthopaedics for a bit of sympathy. Honestly, he was like another child! She shooed him away again, promising to send Swifty to talk to him when he got here from school.

Poor Swifty. His life was a misery. Stuck with Sister Mitchell in her posh, fussy flat, having to put up with her acting like his mother. She'd decided she was against the idea of latchkey kids, and he was under orders to report to the Hospital after school each day and wait for her to take him home. More likely she didn't want him at large in her flat.

Up to now at least he'd had Jamie here, but today bad news awaited him: Jamie was about to go home.

The two were standing discussing it when a voice called Jamie from near by. 'Oy!'

It was the older lad who'd been knocked off his bike. 'Can you collect something for me,' he asked Jamie, 'and bring it back here?'

They went over to him. 'What?' asked Jamie.

'A packet.'

'A packet of what?'

'I can't tell you.'

Jamie frowned. 'Say it's not legal. Say I get done . . .'

'If you get done, I get done . . .'

Jamie shook his head, deciding. 'Nah. I'll have to get going, me dad's waiting.'

Simmo said quickly: 'I'll give you a tenner.'

'We'll do it,' said Swifty, holding his hand out.

Simmo snorted. 'When you've brought the package back – unopened.'

Swifty and Jamie looked at each other, deciding they really would do it.

Half-past four in the afternoon. Sister Mitchell believed that Swifty was at his dad's bedside on Male Orthopaedics, and Swifty's dad was under the blithe impression that Swifty was making himself useful on Sister Mitchell's ward.

In fact he'd already been back home for his bike, and now he and Jamie were speeding along the canal towpath towards the bridge where Simmo said the package was hidden.

They were excited. It was an adventure. 'Geronimo!' they yelled as they clattered along.

'This is it!' Jamie cried, jumping off his bike and throwing it down.

They searched among the bushes, poking and prising the branches aside. Nothing. They were about to give up when Swifty spotted it: the pile of stones against the wall and the corner of the package jutting out. 'Yo!'

He pulled it out. The package felt solid. It was heavily sealed with packing tape.

Suddenly, they were very curious. 'What do you think's in it?' Jamie mused.

'Why don't we open it and have a look?'

'What?!! Simmo'll do his fruit!'

'We won't tell him.'

'You think he won't find out? With all that tape on it?'

'We can tape it up again so he won't know. We can do it at Mitchell's – she's still at Sparkies. And I've got this!' He held up a key. 'I "borrowed" it from my dad's room at home.'

Jamie cried: 'She'll go spare if she finds out!'

'What's new?' And Swifty was already slipping down the canalside and grabbing his bike.

In no time they reached Mitchell's flat, parking their bikes in the shared hall downstairs.

'Wow,' said Jamie, looking around at the posh furniture, the pastel curtains and spotless carpets. They went into the spare room, where Swifty was sleeping and which had already lost its immaculate character.

They sat on the bed and laid the package between them.

'What do you think it is?' said Jamie. 'Secret documents?'

'Drugs?'

'Maybe we shouldn't –'

But Swifty had already begun yanking at the tape.

They couldn't believe their eyes. Through the gaps in the packing bulged ten-pound notes. Wads of them, wrapped in rubber bands.

When they had got over the shock, they counted them out.

'Nine hundred and sixty . . . nine hundred and eighty . . . *one thousand pounds*! A grand! A blinkin' grand!' Swifty cried.

They looked at each other. 'What's Simmo doing with a thousand quid?'

Jamie said grimly, 'It won't be a paper round.'

'Drugs money . . .? Or from a robbery?'

'It can't be legal. Or he wouldn't have stashed it.'

'Anyone could have found it!' Swifty commented.

They looked at each other again. Anyone. Before they got there . . . Simmo wouldn't know any different, if they said it had already gone . . .

They were rich.

'Whooooo!' Swifty yelled, throwing the notes in a great shower into the air.

Back on the ward, Simmo waited in vain.

No one noticed that he was looking worried. Too many others had worries of their own. Sarah came into the ward from the washroom and saw Faye and Dan lolling together, quite drunk. At last she flipped, pointing at Jude. 'Your boyfriend's lying there – or have you forgotten?'

Faye gave a dismissive hiccup: 'You know your problem: you're jealous.'

Sarah snarled: 'Of *you*!!? You must be joking!'

'Leave it out, Sarah,' said Dan, too drunk now to be nasty. 'We were only having a laugh.'

Faye stood up and pushed her face into Sarah's.

'You should try it sometime. Second thoughts, better not, your face might crack.'

Sarah hit her.

Faye grabbed her hair. 'You've been asking for this!' And then the two were grappling, Sarah hampered by her injuries but still putting up a good fight.

Dan sat by, looking stupidly flattered.

Tim was on the spot in no time. 'Break it up.' He got between them and held them apart as the staff arrived on the scene.

Sarah slunk off to her bed, comforted by Keely.

Tim turned to Faye and Dan. 'You two don't give a toss about anyone, do you?'

'On your bike!' Faye snarled at the top of her voice.

As if in answer, a voice said weakly: 'Faye . . .'

They all turned. Jude. The voice had come from Jude . . .

Faye ran to him.

'Jude!' she cried. 'He spoke! Jude!'

But he said nothing more. He simply stared at her blankly. He didn't know her.

Five

Next morning Jude was off his drip and was to be fed a milky purée. Dan watched in horror from his bed as Rob tied a bib round Jude's neck and began to spoon up the milky mixture. As Faye had said, just like a baby. Jude's arms hung, useless, by his sides and he turned his head away, vaguely, towards some sound on the ward. Rob waited until Jude's head was turned in the right direction and then spooned some of the mixture in. Jude screwed his mouth up and spat it out again. All the time Rob was talking to him, murmuring, but getting no response.

Dan turned away.

Dr Gallagher came and examined Dan.

'Great, Dan,' he pronounced finally. 'You're really picking up.'

'Glad you're pleased,' Dan sneered.

Sarah put in: 'His new girlfriend will be.' When Dr Gallagher had gone, she snorted sarcastically. 'Aren't you scared what Jude will say?'

She went over to Jude, whose messy breakfast was over now. He was sitting, propped and staring. She said to him savagely: 'You don't mind, do you, Jude, if he runs off with your girlfriend, eh?'

Jude looked at her vaguely, his mouth hanging.

'You're sick, you!' said Dan, unhappy and disgusted, and he got up and went out.

Sarah looked back at Jude. He was still gazing at her wonderingly. His hair had flopped into his eyes. Gently she pushed it back again, swallowing on the lump in her throat.

Simmo watched the door anxiously. Where were those kids with the package?

The girls near by were getting on his nerves, giggling and fussing about some trap they'd laid to catch a thief, which hadn't worked. And some practical joke: one of them, that Tanya, had woken up with her plaster carefully wallpapered. And the nurses were just as bad.

Keely had been telling Martin off for leaving his materials lying around overnight.

'Aye-aye!' Diane commented knowingly, sidling up to Keely after he'd gone. 'You were flirting with him!'

'I was not!' Keely was laughing, a little pink.

Diane smirked cynically.

'It was nerves. Exam results come out today, remember.'

*

During her morning tea-break, Sandra Mitchell went to visit Tom on the Male Ward. They were allowing him home today, but he was still feeling sorry for himself. 'I've still got this twinge . . .' he moaned.

He didn't get much sympathy from Sandra; something else was concerning her. 'Tom . . .?' she asked. 'How much pocket-money does Sean get?'

Tom looked at her in surprise, and without much interest, still holding his back. 'A fiver. And his mother sends him money sometimes. And his grandma . . .' He laughed. 'Come to think of it, he does better than I do. Why?'

She was frowning, and looking a little awkward. 'Well, I found two ten-pound notes under his bed this morning.'

After Sean had left for school she had looked into his room, unable to believe her eyes at the mess he'd managed to make in three days: clothes strewn everywhere, dirty cereal bowls on the floor with their contents congealing . . . She had bent to pick some of them up, and had seen the two notes lying curled beneath the bed, almost as if Sean had money to throw away . . .

So why did he say he needed the bus fare for school? And then she'd remembered how, when she'd asked him if he did, a strange look had crossed his face. As if he was deciding he'd better not confess to having any money at all . . .

Tom laughed at her suspicions. 'You don't know children, Sandra. Bus Fare Money and New School Shoes Money is completely separate from money you spend on computer games and quarter-pounders.'

And that was another thing. Those plastic bags she'd found stuffed under the bed, new-smelling and bearing the name of a computer shop . . . She said no more to Tom for now, but she had a worried feeling that, even though Swifty had money to scatter, he'd already done some expensive shopping late yesterday afternoon.

In any case, she'd cleared up his room, the plastic bags and dirty pots, and stacked up all his old comics for the recycling centre. Which was just as well since if Tom was going home, Sean would be moving out this evening . . .

Tom was saying: 'It's still really painful . . .' He was looking at her beseechingly. 'I don't know how I'm going to cope with Sean . . .'

She groaned inwardly.

'I don't even think I could cope on my own . . .'

She gave in. 'All right. You can come and stay with me until you've made a full recovery.'

He broke into a grateful grin.

She said quickly: 'Certain house rules, though: no football on the telly and no sweaty socks under the bed, for a start.'

His grin froze. 'I say, Sandra,' he cried in dismay,

'for a qualified nurse you have a very poor bedside manner.'

It was school lunch-hour. Swifty and Jamie were on their way into the hospital, rehearsing what they were going to say to Simmo.

Swifty said: 'Now remember: *We looked everywhere. In all the bushes.*'

'Yes, for an hour.'

'But we couldn't find it anywhere.'

'Someone must have picked it up.'

'So anyway, Simmo, we haven't got it.'

They had reached the ward entrance. Jamie stopped in dread. 'What if he doesn't believe us?'

Swifty rolled his eyes. 'Just stick to the story and we're quids in.' And he swung purposefully into the ward.

'So, anyway, Simmo, we haven't got it.'

Swifty finished their tale cheerfully.

There was a silence. Simmo was glowering. He lunged suddenly forward, grabbing hold of Jamie's bandaged hand.

'Get off him!' Swifty cried.

Simmo held on, and Jamie gasped in pain. 'Listen, you pair. I've had about enough of this. Just give me that packet.'

'We haven't got it!' Jamie gasped.

'No, honest,' Swifty protested, 'we haven't got your money.'

He froze. He'd given it away. Simmo's eyes narrowed. He threw Jamie's hand away from him, making him wince again. 'I want it today.'

What were they going to do? They'd already spent some of it. Swifty let them into Mitchell's flat. They'd been too anxious and preoccupied to go back to school.

They tried to work out how much they'd spent. There were the computer games, they knew how much they'd been, but what about the rest? They'd just started splashing it around . . .

'We had those burgers, remember – that must have been about six quid . . .'

That accounted for £89. But was that all of it? And how on earth could they get it back again?

Swifty suggested wildly: 'We could take the computer games back. Say they were faulty.'

'They weren't.'

'We could make them – break the cartridges . . .?'

Jamie shook his head. His heart had never really been in this, anyway. He was getting fed up with Swifty – he just didn't live in the real world.

'Have you got any money in the bank?' Swifty asked hopefully.

'You must be joking!' The only money Jamie had ever had was what he'd once earned in the laundry where he injured his hand, and that had gone to keep the family because his dad couldn't work.

Jamie felt miserable. He looked around the plush flat. There was so much money about here. And Swifty's dad looked like he was rolling in it, he was an architect or something . . . For people like that, life was just one big laugh, they had no idea . . . Swifty didn't even need those computer games, he had plenty already, scattered all over his room. Yet it was Swifty who'd been greedy and got them into this scrape. More than just a scrape . . . Jamie's hand was still throbbing where Simmo had grabbed hold and deliberately squeezed . . . Jamie said mournfully: 'What about asking your dad?'

'I can't just ask him for a hundred quid, he'd have to know what for. And before you say it – there's no point in asking Mitchell!'

Swifty scratched his head.

'We'd better work out how much we *really* need. Count how much we've got left.' He went into his room to get the packet from where he'd hidden it, in the middle of the pile of comics under the bed.

'Oh no!'

The room was transformed. Everything tidied. There was nothing left beneath the bed. The comics were nowhere to be seen, and the package was gone.

Kieran was saying to Sandra: 'I know Swifty's a handful, but he isn't a *bad* kid.'

Over afternoon tea-break she was voicing her vague worries about him to the other staff She smiled. Kieran could always be guaranteed to take the child's side.

Mags commiserated with her. 'I bet you thought you were getting a rest, and now you're going to have two of them! Next thing, you'll be coming in to work for a rest!'

Sandra grimaced. 'What, with Faye on the ward?'

They all rolled their eyes.

Sandra said: 'You know, Kieran, I've been thinking: perhaps you could have a word with her?'

'What, *me*?' As if he hadn't tried. With his boyish manner and his special rapport with kids, it was usually Kieran who could get through to them, but this lot had him stumped. They'd been determined to keep him firmly in the camp of boring old stiff. He was starting to feel like one. He could hear through their ears the pompousness of his words as he tried to get through . . .

'Huh!' Mags was saying. 'I shouldn't bother talking to her. Just tell her she can't come in any more!'

Sandra went on: 'She's got to realize this is unacceptable. She's a manipulator, Kieran. If we don't put her straight, there's going to be bedlam on this ward.'

'All right, I'll try,' said Kieran, without much conviction.

*

Faye had just arrived on the ward.

She came in and hovered in the entrance, stirring it, waiting for Dan and Sarah to notice her.

They looked up. She saw them both look expectant, waiting to see what she would do. She gave Dan a dazzling smile, registered his smile back and Sarah's hurt expression, then she flicked her hair, turned away from them and went and sat at Jude's bed.

Dan was watching her and she smiled back.

In disgust and hurt, Sarah got up and went and joined Stiff Tim and the giggly brat girls.

Faye tossed her hair back. She caught sight of Jude. He was dribbling. She felt sick.

And then Gallagher was at her side, all eager and encouraging and palsy-walsy. That was all she needed.

'Hard work, eh, when you're getting nothing back,' he said. Assuming she'd been talking to this dribbling . . . *thing*. As if it was anything to do with *her* . . . Or anything to do with Jude . . . She felt even sicker.

Gallagher was babbling on: 'Your best bet's reading to him. He gets stimulation and you feel like you're doing something. Doesn't matter what. Even computer books if you can stand it.'

Pious git. She said scornfully, 'He never went in for *reading* much.'

He sat down beside her. 'Funny. We do everything we can for the patient, but no one ever thinks about the family or the boyfriend or girlfriend, about telling them what to do –'

She snapped: 'I don't need *telling* what to do! I don't need telling that that's not Jude!'

He bent towards her, earnest. 'Listen, Faye, just 'cos he can't express himself doesn't mean his brain's packed in altogether. There's always hope. He could make a complete recovery for all we know.'

She challenged: 'And then again, he might not, right?'

Gallagher looked awkward. He wasn't denying it. 'He needs encouragement and all the attention he can get.'

She sneered, suddenly angry. 'Oh, I get it. Be a good girl and he might get better. Well, it's not up to me!'

'You can drop the act with me, Faye. I know you care about Jude, or you wouldn't be in here, day in, day out.'

'Well, I don't come in for the crack!' she sneered. She was defiant. 'I've got other mates here.'

'Yes, and it leads to too much fighting. Leave the boxing gloves at home from now on, yeah?' Then he dropped his own act and said stiffly: 'Remember, I could stop you coming here.'

He was as bad as the rest of them. Because he tried to pretend he was so cool, he was one of the worst.

*

Over at Debbie's bed, Sarah had found Tim and the girls playing Monopoly. 'D'you want anything from the drinks machine?' she asked them.

'I'll come with you,' said Tim, putting the dice down.

As they put the money in, he asked her: 'Aren't your mates talking to you any more?'

She shook her head, trying to grin.

'That boyfriend of yours isn't any great loss.' He paused, pressing the buttons on the machine. Then he said: 'You could do better.'

He was looking hard at her.

She blushed and looked away, feeling suddenly not so bad after all.

Tanya went home, waving a giggly goodbye to Martin.

Two newcomers arrived together: a boy and a girl dressed in leather and holding hands. At thirteen, Mel was a good few inches taller than her twelve-year-old boyfriend, Wiggy, and it was quite clear which of the two was boss. It was Mel who set up a protest when they discovered that they couldn't be near each other on the ward.

'Sorry, lovey,' Mags said briskly, changing Tanya's bed for her. 'You have to take what's free.'

Keely and Sandra Mitchell peeled the bandages off the infections which had been the cause of their coming into hospital.

'Oh no!' Keely cried, unable to stop herself as the skin on their arms was revealed. They were home-made tattoos, badly infected, the skin round them blistered and red. It was an old and familiar sight to her: at fifteen she had been brought here with one of these and had become very ill, developing hepatitis.

Mel and Wiggy, however, were admiring their handiwork, each sporting the other's name. Mel announced airily: 'It's only like getting your ears pierced.'

'Cellulitis,' Sandra Mitchell informed Keely. 'So we'll be giving antibiotic injections.'

Mel looked a bit less confident. 'What's that mean?'

Keely grinned. 'In your bum. *Only like getting your ears pierced.*'

Sandra Mitchell told them seriously: 'You two have got off very lightly. You could have caught hepatitis. Or even passed on HIV from sharing the needle.'

Mel was shocked. 'We're not tramps!'

Sister Mitchell gave brief instructions to Keely, then she glanced at Mel's locker and array of hair gels and make-up. 'Oh, Mel. I think you'll find while you're in hospital you won't need to wear quite so much make-up.'

'What a bag!' Mel exclaimed when she'd gone.

'Now, now,' Keely admonished.

'Well, I don't go around telling her not to wear American Tan tights with black shoes!'

Keely couldn't help but smile. She'd been just the same herself as a teenage patient: plastering on the make-up and dispensing hairdressing tips round the ward. 'I've got a tattoo,' she told Mel. 'Biggest mistake of my life.'

'Why?' Mel asked in amazement.

'Well, why do I want the name of some lad I've not seen for years on me arm?'

Mel looked superior. 'Well, yes, a tattoo's for keeps. You have to be sure of each other.'

'Oh, so how long have you two been going out together?' Keely asked, amused.

'Eight weeks,' they said proudly, in unison.

Dan and Faye were sitting one on each side of the chair in which Jude had now been strapped. They were in a wicked, hilarious mood. 'Like talking to a parrot, innit?' Faye said about Jude, referring to the way he had said her name last night. Dan grinned. 'Hey,' she said, 'we could teach him all sorts.' She turned to Jude. 'Jude?' He looked at her slowly, his eyeballs focusing the way those of babies in prams do. She said to him with exaggerated slowness, 'Say: "Sister Mitchell's a snotty old bag."' Jude watched her, moving his head, possibly in echo of her movements, possibly not. 'Go on: "Sister Mitchell . . ."'

Dan was grinning.

Jude was silent. 'Nah,' she said dismissively. 'Lost his bottle.'

She caught sight of the grapes on Jude's locker, sent by someone who didn't know that Jude couldn't eat solid food. She held them up in ridicule. 'We'll have to give him a hand.'

'I'm not supposed to mix with you,' she told Dan scornfully as they tucked into them.

'Why not?' he asked in mock innocence, his cheeks crammed with grapes.

''Cos you talk with your mouth full!'

He spat a grape-pip at her, and she spat one back. And then they were spitting and throwing them, over the bed, not noticing that Jude flinched whenever they hit him in the face.

Some time after they'd left Jude, Leanne was standing all alone in the ward entrance. She had sneaked out of school and made her way back here by bus. She had figured it out: whatever she said, her parents weren't going to let her see him, so there was nothing for it but to come again on her own, at a time when she knew they wouldn't be here.

She looked around.

And there he was, sitting up in a big chair, looking away from her down the ward.

She went over excitedly. 'Hiya, Jude!'

He turned to look at her. His head lolled. His eyes gazed at her blankly.

'Jude?' she asked uncertainly. Her chest started banging. He stared right through her.

She ran from the ward and into the arms of Nurse Gallagher.

'Why won't he speak to me?' she cried, staring at him.

Kieran and Diane had brought her back to Jude's side. Diane was now stroking his hand.

Kieran explained gently: 'He's had a very serious accident – you know that, don't you? Because it was such a nasty bump on the head it's made him forget a lot of things.'

Diane asked: 'Do you want to come and sit down by him?'

She hung back, afraid, but after a moment she approached. As she did so, Jude gave a great jerk in his chair, and she jumped in fright and horror.

'Don't worry,' Diane reassured her. 'He does that sometimes.'

She caught sight of something on Jude's bed. 'Is that a nappy?'

Diane said gently: 'It's a kind of nappy for people who are too poorly to look after themselves. When you've been as ill as he has, it's a bit like being a baby. You have to learn everything all over again.'

Leanne looked at Jude's vacant face. He *did* look a bit like a baby, the way he stared.

'Would you like to hold his other hand?'

For a moment she thought she couldn't, but then she reached out and took it. Its feel was familiar. Long and bony and warm. The hand she held when he took her swimming . . .

She squeezed it tight.

Swifty and Jamie had looked everywhere in the flat. The comics had gone completely, and with them the package.

There was nothing for it but to go and ask Mitchell what she'd done with them.

'Sean!' she cried as he came into the office. 'You should be at school!'

'Er . . . there was a fire alarm!' And before she could question him further, he demanded anxiously: 'Where are my comics?'

She folded her arms, as if ready to do battle. 'That bedroom looked as if a bomb had hit it.' She stopped, as realization dawned. 'How do you know I've tidied up?'

He looked sheepish.

She asked ominously, 'How did you get into the flat?'

He confessed.

She held her hand out for the key, and he was forced to give it up. She was most displeased. 'This is serious,' she told him, putting the key in her handbag.'

Good job she didn't know just *how* serious . . .

'I'm sorry,' he mumbled, and then looked up anxiously. 'Where are my comics?'

She sighed. 'In the car, ready to be taken to the recycling depot.'

'Oh, right!' His face lit up in relief and he was gone.

She sighed again.

Jamie cried: 'But how are we going to get it out of the car?'

Swifty hadn't thought about that.

They looked worriedly through the ward doors towards Simmo, sitting hunched in his bed.

Swifty would have to get the car keys out of Mitchell's handbag. They hung around and, as soon as the office was empty, Swifty dived in. He had just got her handbag open when the phone on the desk began to ring. Lookout Jamie banged a warning that Kieran was coming to answer it, and Swifty got out just in time. He hadn't managed to get the keys.

What now?

A man and a woman sat down on Simmo's bed and the three began talking intently. Swifty and Jamie could guess about what . . .

'No toffees today, love,' Cath Wilson was saying nastily to Simmo. 'Because we knew you'd have a pressie for *us*.'

'I haven't got it.' Simmo was aggressive and scared.

Cath's lips tightened. She leaned forward. 'This explanation had better be good.'

Bernard shifted threateningly in his chair.

At that moment, two brats were accosting Dan in the corridor just outside the main ward. 'Hey, Dan!'

He shook his head to make them shift, but they stood their ground.

Swifty said: 'We need a favour.'

He almost laughed. 'How much?' he sneered.

They sighed. 'Five quid,' they offered, forfeiting yet more of the money.

They were serious. Curious, he listened.

Out in the car park, they fidgeted anxiously while he did his best to pick the lock of Mitchell's car.

'Get a move on!' Swifty hissed.

'Chill out,' he complained. 'I've done me arm in, haven't I? I'm bound to take a bit longer.'

Up in the office, Sandra Mitchell noticed her handbag open. She checked the contents, but nothing had gone. 'Someone's definitely been in it,' she told Kieran.

They were troubled. Missing toys, and now this . . . Looked like there *was* a thief on the ward . . .

*

The car door clicked open.

'Yesss!' Dan watched, amused, as Swifty and Jamie went scrabbling through the boxes of comics.

'Oy – fiver!' he reminded them.

'Yeah, when we find it.' And at that very moment they did. Swifty grabbed the package and held it up triumphantly.

Now Dan was really interested. He reached over with his good arm and swiped the package off the shrimp.

Jamie and Swifty were dismayed, panicking, and Dan looked to see what they were so sorry to lose. He couldn't believe his eyes: where the package was torn, wads of ten-pound notes were revealed. He held it over their heads.

'Hey, give it back,' they shouted, jumping, and he waved it, making them dance.

'No way.' He tutted. 'And I did that car for a fiver!' High up, he began to slide the notes out, fingering them.

'Don't!' Swifty cried. 'It's not our money!'

'You surprise me!' he sneered. Out of casual interest he asked, 'So whose is it?'

'Simmo's.'

He flung it back at them as if it had stung him. 'Forget it. Simmo? He's bad news.'

Now they were really scared.

*

On the ward, Cath was saying to Simmo: 'So we'll have to get it out of you other ways.'

Bernard cracked his fingers.

Simmo said in panic: 'I sent two kids to look for it. They said they couldn't find it.'

Cath's eyes narrowed, only half believing him, and she started looking around. 'Who?'

'Called Swifty and Jamie. I think one of them's the snotty Sister's lad.'

At that moment Nurse Diane Gallagher came up. 'Excuse me, Mr and Mrs Simmondson, Paul's due to see the doctor. Would you like to go and have a cup of tea? We won't be long.'

Grudgingly, Cath and Bernard went off to the waiting room as the doctor arrived and Nurse Gallagher drew the curtains.

In the toilets, Swifty and Jamie miserably braced themselves to take the money to Simmo. So much of it gone, and the package hopelessly torn . . .

And if even Dan didn't like to mess with Simmo, what hope was there for *them*?

They swallowed hard and shuffled into the ward.

The curtains were drawn round Simmo's bed. They went and stood outside them, listening. No sound came from the other side, so he must be sitting there alone.

Swifty took a deep breath and went in.

The bed was empty.

There was nothing in the locker.

Simmo had gone.

'He's scarpered!'

They looked at each other. 'Does this mean we're off the hook?'

In the waiting area Cath was getting impatient. She could see down the ward that the curtains were still drawn round Simmo's bed. 'I'm going to find out what's keeping them.' She marched on to the ward.

She yanked back Simmo's curtains and found what Swifty and Jamie had found: the bed abandoned.

She turned on her glittering heel. 'The little . . .'

In the entrance she caught sight of the Sister leaving. She had two kids tagging along behind her.

'Right,' she told Bernard. 'It's all we've got to go on. We'll have to get those two kids.'

And they started to follow.

Six

Sandra Mitchell drew up at traffic lights, driving Jamie and Swifty home.

'Left after three streets,' Jamie instructed politely from the back.

Another car pulled up alongside, an XR3. Swifty glanced at it in appreciation, then he froze in horror. At the wheel was the woman who'd been talking to Simmo. And even as Swifty spotted her, she was pointing him out to the man in the passenger seat beside her . . .

'It's next left!' said Swifty to Sandra in panic.

'What . . . Are you sure . . . Is that right, Jamie?'

Swifty shot Jamie an urgent look.

'Er . . . yes . . .' Jamie couldn't work out what was going on.

Sandra turned.

To Swifty's dismay, the car turned after them.

They took the tortuous route on to Jamie's estate, and all the way the car followed. There were moments when it seemed they'd lost them, but then their pursuers would nose round the corner after them.

As he turned to look, the package shifted inside his jacket.

They pulled up outside the rusting gate of Jamie's house. At that moment the other car was nowhere in sight. Swifty jumped out with Jamie and pushed the car door to, so that Sandra wouldn't hear. He hissed, 'Simmo's mob are on to us for the dosh!'

'Eh?'

Sandra leaned over and pushed the door open. 'Come on, Sean, we haven't got all day. I've got to go back and pick up Tom at six-thirty.'

Jamie still hadn't understood the warning. With a worried shrug Swifty got back in the car and Sandra drove away.

Just as Jamie was shutting his front door behind him, Cath Wilson and Bernard came nosing into the street, catching up. All they saw was Sandra Mitchell's car turning a corner ahead. Cath put her foot down again and followed.

It was some time before the staff realized that Simmo had gone.

'Oh, brilliant!' Kieran groaned. 'That's all we need!'

It must have been not long after his parents were

here . . . Kieran rushed to the phone to warn them, hoping they'd be home by now. While he was waiting for the call to connect, he told Keely, 'He should be on bed rest, not trying to get around on that ankle . . .' He took the phone away from his ear in dismay. 'Unobtainable.'

After a few minutes' investigation it was clear: there was no such phone number. And no such address as the one written in his case notes. The details he had given them were false.

'What they doing, breaking out, if this place is so great?' Mel demanded of Wiggy, aggressively chewing her gum in irritation. He had sorely disappointed her by finding it not so bad – he'd even said he liked the food! At this rate, he was in danger of turning into a stiff.

She blew a big bubble and it burst with an insolent smack.

And there was discord elsewhere: trouble was brewing between Dan and Sarah and Tim. Faye had made herself scarce when Gallagher turned up again, wanting to avoid another lecture, so now Dan was turning his attention to Sarah and Tim. Debbie was up now, and they were sitting with her at the centre table. As he passed by with a cup of orange, Dan sneered at Tim: 'Wasting your time with that one,' referring to Sarah.

'Shut your face, you!' Sarah snapped.

'See?' Dan smiled with exaggerated blandness at Tim. 'Ignorant.'

Tim stood up. 'And you're just a failed car thief.' He tapped the cup in Dan's hand. It was only a little tap, but Dan was holding it in the weakened hand of his injured arm, and it slipped from his grasp. Yellow liquid spilt down the front of his trousers.

'Whoops,' Tim sneered. 'Better tell Nursey you've wet yourself.'

At that moment Mags was passing. 'Ooh, Dan, look at you!' she exclaimed and came towards him to help.

'Get off, will you!' he said roughly, knocking her away.

Now Dan really wanted out of here.

The next person to get the edge of Dan's temper was Rob, who came to give him his physio and, as soon as he'd finished, was faced with an aggressive demand: 'Well?'

'Well what?'

'Is it improving? When can I go home?'

'Better ask the doctor. It's not up to us.' Rob was preoccupied; in not much more than an hour, at the end of the day, the exam results would be pinned up.

He made to open Dan's curtains and leave.

Dan took objection to what he thought was Rob's dismissive attitude. He stood up in front of him. 'I'm talking to you.'

He was threatening. He was blocking Rob's exit; the curtains were still drawn and no one could see them. He was easily Rob's height. Rob reached for the curtain. 'I'm busy.'

Dan practically spat. 'Busy doing what, making beds and mopping up spew?'

Rob said drily: 'Something like that. There are other children on this ward.' He paused and added significantly: 'Besides you.' And he whipped the curtains open.

'Get real, will you,' Dan said furiously. 'I don't need to be in here, I'm not a kid and I'm not a cripple. I shouldn't be in here.'

Rob said with cool irony, 'Well, I'll be sure to pass your comments on to Dr Gallagher. Have a nice day now.'

Now Dan was really rattled.

Leanne was still here, waiting for her father, whom they'd rung.

It was time for Jude's tea. She watched solemnly as Diane tied on his bib.

'Would you like to feed him?' Diane asked.

She wasn't sure, but she felt she ought to. She should do it for Jude . . .

She took the spoon filled with porridge. Nervously, she moved it towards his mouth. He opened his mouth, ready, and took it eagerly.

'Good!' said Diane, to both of them.

It was easy. She took the bowl and gave him another spoonful.

He spat it out, all over her hand.

She jumped back in disgust: she couldn't bear it. She threw the spoon and the bowl away from her, and they landed all over Jude's lap.

Mr Latimer, arriving in that moment, rushed to their side.

'It's horrible!' Leanne cried, flinging herself at him. 'Look at him, he's like a big baby!'

Mr Latimer was torn between Leanne and his son behind her, covered in porridge and gurgling in distress.

Mr Latimer looked up and into the eyes of Faye, standing solemnly watching them.

Leanne caught sight of Faye. 'Faye!' she cried, and disentangled herself from her father, and went across. 'He doesn't recognize me! Does he recognize you?'

Faye shook her head, and Leanne sobbed. Over her head Faye could see what had happened: the porridge everywhere, and Diane clearing it up; the cause of Leanne's horror and disgust, which she understood so well. And Jude's distress . . .

Suddenly Faye wanted to cry too.

Mr Latimer came over and put a protective hand on Leanne.

Faye looked up at him. 'Mr Latimer . . . I'm sorry . . .'

He looked at her coolly.

She faltered. 'All that stuff I said. Especially to Mrs Latimer . . . I'm sorry –'

He cut her off, saying coldly: 'If you want to prove how sorry you are, just keep out of our way. And don't feel you have to keep visiting Jude out of guilt.' And he propelled Leanne away from her, out of the hospital.

Faye beckoned for Dan to come out of the ward and sit under the stairs.

'What's with this?' Dan wanted to know.

'Don't want another lecture, do I?' She was chewing madly at her gum, preoccupied. She was as wound up as he was. No way was she setting foot in that ward again tonight.

'This place is doing my head in,' he was telling her. 'Least at school I didn't have Sarah in me face twenty-four hours a day. And the staff on your back, treating you like a three-year-old. Least Simmo did a bunk. You should have been here.'

She was hardly listening. She said suddenly: 'I'm thinking of going over to Blackpool. Tonight.' She looked at him challengingly. 'Coming?'

'I'm in hospital, I can't just walk out!'

Her lip curled as she chewed. 'You said Simmo did.'

He was shamed. He said quickly: 'They're cracking down after that. Go next week, eh? I'll be out then.'

But she'd already stood up.

She looked him over for a moment, chewing. Then she said in contempt: 'See you round, Dan,' and was gone.

'Short but sweet.' Sarah's voice, triumphant and scornful. She had been standing, watching the whole thing.

She flounced off. He sat, clenching his hands, furious with everyone.

When he went back into the ward, she was flirting with Tim again.

Tim was teasing Ellie, who had asked if he had a girlfriend. 'Me, I've got loads!'

Sarah shrieked: 'They must be desperate!'

'You can talk!' This was a dig at Dan as he approached.

'Yeah, well, we all make mistakes, don't we?' Sarah said loudly and airily, for Dan's benefit.

Nurse Gallagher came up to them with six-year-old Heather on her hand, re-admitted at long last. 'This is Heather, everyone.'

She looked up at them all, frightened, her bunches trembling.

Ellie sidled around to her. 'You've been in before, haven't you?'

'Yes!' replied Heather, nervous but earnest. 'But some naughty boys came and took my bed.'

'Now I wonder who that was?' Tim said significantly, with a sidelong look at Dan.

Diane Gallagher said quickly, 'Well, I'm sure Ellie will show you around.' Eager to oblige, Ellie took her hand, and led her off to the Day Room.

'Where'd they find her?' Mel commented through a burst bubble of gum, 'Little House on the Prairie?'

And Diane couldn't help but smile in agreement. Ten minutes after she'd left Heather, having told her to put her nightie on, Diane had returned to find her indeed wearing her nightie, but sitting sedately on her bed with her coat on over the top of it and buttoned wrongly, and still wearing her socks and shoes. In one hand she was clutching her teddy and in the other her overnight bag, in expectation of being sent home once again.

'You're daft, you!' Diane had smiled, bending to take her coat off again, and she promised that this time Heather really wouldn't be turfed out again.

If anyone could make her feel at home, it would be Ellie. Diane had never known a child settle in so well. When Kieran had told Ellie this morning that since all her tests were negative they'd be sending her home soon, Diane could have sworn that Ellie looked dismayed . . .

She went for a check around. The workmen were clearing up now, and she could see that after this morning's accusations, they were locking up carefully and seeing that nothing was left lying around.

And Keely and Rob were just off to get the

results of their exams. 'Good luck!' she called, and they pulled faces of dread.

Student nurses were swarming near the notice-board.

Keely pushed her way through, leaving Rob behind. She couldn't wait one moment longer to find out whether it had all been worth while – keeping going when a thousand times she could have given up: swotting till late at night then having to wake up with Lauren, never going out, braving Billy's doubts that she should be doing it, and half the time seeming to prove him right . . . and the rows between them that all the stresses had caused . . .

She scanned the list: it swam in front of her eyes. Then they latched on to her own name: KEELY JOHNSON . . . She followed the line along . . .

She had passed.

'I've passed!' She swirled backwards and flung herself into Rob's arms in joy.

She felt his tenseness; he hadn't dared to look yet.

She dragged him over to the board.

They saw it together: he had failed.

Back at Sandra Mitchell's flat, Swifty was at the window, gazing anxiously at the road down below.

Cath Wilson's car was parked down there. They were watching the flat.

He pulled back so they wouldn't see him.

Sandra was busy, making preparations for Tom's arrival. 'Right, that's that,' she pronounced. 'Just got time to have a shower.' She noticed him at the window and realized that he wasn't acting like his usual self. 'What's the matter? We've been home more than half an hour, and you haven't switched the telly on!'

At that moment the car pulled away and moved off out of the road. 'Given up!' he breathed aloud.

Sandra raised her eyebrows. 'Given up *telly*?' But she didn't have time to muse. 'While I'm in the shower, would you peel the potatoes, please?'

She had expected a protest but, full of relief at the turn in events, Swifty agreed willingly.

It was when he was on his third potato that the ring came at the doorbell.

'Get that, would you, Sean!' Sandra called from the hissing shower.

He put down the knife, wiped his hands and went uneasily along the corridor. He opened up.

Cath Wilson pushed into the opening. 'Swifty, isn't it?' Her smile glittered; her eyes were hard with menace.

'Sandra!' Swifty called in panic.

Cath snapped: 'Don't be stupid, lad,' and then her voice softened slyly: 'I'm not going to do owt to you.'

'Sandra!' he called again. 'It's for you!'

He never thought he'd feel so relieved to have Mitch on the scene.

'Who is it?' she asked coolly, coming up behind him in her dressing-gown, wrapping a towel round her head.

Cath gave her an oily smile, her bright lipstick glistening. 'I'm sorry to bother you, love. It's not you I was after. I've got the wrong flat.'

Sandra said crisply: 'You're Paul Simmondson's mother, aren't you?'

There was only a split second's hesitation before Cath gushed, 'That's right!' She turned to Swifty. '*You* know my Paul, don't you?' Her tone was friendly, excessively friendly, and because she was looking down at him and not at Sandra, only Swifty saw the threat flashing in her eyes.

'No!' he said, frightened.

Then, to his dismay, Sandra put in almost eagerly, 'Yes, you do. He's on B1. Simmo. I've seen you talking to him.'

'That's right. You *do* know him,' Cath insisted. 'He's only fifteen, but he's big for his age. And *stupid sometimes*.' She looked hard at Swifty, making sure he got the message. 'Has it clicked yet?' She asked it lightly, but he knew what she meant.

'I think so,' he said in misery.

Sandra was in a hurry and she'd had enough of this idle chatter. 'So, which flat were you looking for?'

'Oh, it's all right, love, I know where I am now! Ta-ra.' She stepped away as Sandra nodded goodbye, and Swifty shut the door.

As Sandra went back to the bathroom, he slipped the chain on the door.

When she emerged from her bedroom with her car keys, he was ready to go with her. She was surprised. 'I'll only be gone ten minutes.'

He thought quickly. 'But you don't like me being in the flat on my own!'

She smirked good-naturedly. She'd relaxed on that one. Theory was all very well, but once you were faced with the practicalities of looking after children . . . 'Look, I need you to keep an eye on the dinner. And anyway, I want to call in at the ward to see how the exam results went. Could you set the table?' She smiled as she went out through the door.

Distraught, he quickly put the chain back on behind her.

In the car outside, Cath Wilson and Bernard saw Sandra Mitchell leave the entrance to the flats and get into her car.

'Aye-aye!' said Cath with satisfaction.

As Sandra drove off, they both got out and made their way towards the flats.

On B1, staff were full of the news of the exam results. Rob was nowhere to be seen. Keely was upset, the edge taken off her own success. 'I don't believe it,' she told Mags in the kitchen, shaking her head. 'Unless he did less work than he said.'

To her horror, at that moment Rob appeared in the doorway and he must have heard. 'Message from the kitchen staff,' he told Mags impassively. 'They want their trolley back as soon as poss.'

'Right, love,' said Mags, too eagerly and sympathetically, and he turned away quickly.

'Rob –' Keely called out in concern.

He turned back. 'Just forget it, Keely. It's no big deal.'

And they let him go, leaving him to his pride.

Just as well, because then the rest of the staff piled in to congratulate Keely, even Sandra, coming in specially with Tom in tow. Keely grinned, flattered and pleased.

Under cover of the diversion, Dan sauntered to the decorator's cupboard in the corridor. He looked right and left, making sure no one was around, then began to pick the lock. The cupboard door swung open. He was becoming quite deft at doing things one-handed. He picked up a paintbrush and a tin of black paint. He got the paint tin open. He surveyed the newly painted wall, choosing his spot. He dipped the paintbrush in and began . . .

All unawares, the staff chatted on.

'Stay for a celebratory cuppa?' Mags asked Sandra and Tom.

Sandra looked at her watch. 'We'd better get back to Sean.'

'Before he burns the flat down,' Tom added.

'Gerraway! Five minutes won't kill you.'

They sat down.

In the excitement, no one thought to tell Sandra about the events concerning the Simmondsons while she'd been gone . . .

As soon as Sandra left the flat, Swifty went round shutting all the windows. His heart was thumping. He drew the curtains, so he didn't see Bernard step round the side of the flats and position himself below a window.

The telephone rang. Swifty jumped, his skin prickling. He stared at it and backed away. He sat cowering on the sofa, waiting for it to stop. He turned the TV up loud to drown its sound.

The ringing suddenly cut off.

Half a mile away, Jamie came out of a phone box, scratching his head and wondering if the note he'd got of Sister Mitchell's number was wrong . . .

Under the ringing of the phone and the booming of the TV, Swifty had failed to hear the footsteps coming up the stairs and crossing the landing to the flat door.

Mel came into the ward and faced Sarah out. 'You lot make me laugh. You slag us off for getting tattoos, but we're not flamin' vandals. Seen what your sad boyfriend's done out there?' She meant Tim. 'I'd bin him if I were you.'

Sarah looked at him, but he only shrugged, he didn't know what Mel was going on about.

With a terrible sense of foreboding, Sarah went to see.

SARAH LUVS TIM was sprawled in bright black paint on the newly decorated corridor wall. The kids came crowding around to look and, aware of the commotion, staff came spilling out of the kitchen.

There it was, for all to see, and everyone was looking . . .

The last to see it was Tim. He took one look at it, and his face tightened.

Sarah looked at him beseechingly, willing him to know that she hadn't done it, that she hated it.

He turned away from her, anger and embarrassment turning his ears red, and went back into the ward.

In sheer humiliation, she ran to the toilets to hide.

Sandra Mitchell turned fiercely on Dan. 'This stops. Now.'

He jumped, surprised by her ferocity. A few others were surprised, including members of staff. Momentarily, Dan collected his cool. 'What you looking at me for?'

She pushed towards him. He felt cornered. 'Cut the backchat.' She pushed her face into his. 'I haven't always worked on this ward. I've done my stint on Casualty. I've seen the likes of you, ten years on, getting carried in, every Saturday night, with broken ribs and stab wounds, and much worse. You know the gang mentality. All these grand gestures ever get you is a good kicking.' They were eyeball to eyeball. She sneered. 'You carry on doing what the gang expects if that's what you want to do. *But not on my ward.*' She stood back.

He slunk off, stunned.

Everyone was staring at her. Kieran raised an eyebrow. Seemed like she'd got a knack he'd never managed with his softly-softly approach.

'I say, Sandra!' Tom said in adoring admiration.

She gathered up her handbag and walked crisply away, leaving him to follow.

Swifty was cowering behind the door. The doorbell went on and on. Someone was leaning on it. And now there was a crack as something hit the glass of the window at the back. He jumped as the letter box snapped open above his head. He sprang away. Cath's voice came through the gap. 'Are you there, Swifty? Come on, open up, love. It'll only take a minute.' She was wheedling now.

Too late: Swifty was in sheer terror.

Another crack at the back, and then Cath's voice again: 'Come on, I just want to ask you summat.'

Whimpering, Swifty scrabbled away from the door and ran to the phone. He dialled Sparkies, his hands shaking with terror. He'd just got through when he heard a bang in the hall below. He was beside himself now. 'Yes. Sister Mitchell,' he told the duty officer. 'Tell her to come home!'

There was a loud crack as the flat door was opened and got caught by the chain. He opened his mouth to scream.

'Sean!' came his father's voice. 'Open up!'

'Open the door!' Sandra called. And he never thought he'd be so relieved to hear her voice.

Seven

He poured out his story, telling them everything that had happened, too terrified now to care what they'd say.

They tried to calm him down. Cath and Bernard must have gone: there was no one out there when Sandra and Tom had come home. But Swifty was sure that they'd simply scarpered for the moment and that they would be back to get him under cover of night.

He showed them the money.

Sandra's heart sank. This was more serious than she would ever have guessed. She'd not been a policeman's wife for nothing, and she knew what it could mean. 'You realize this is probably drugs money, don't you?' And being the ex-wife of a policeman, she knew full well the kind of the world upon which Swifty had stumbled, out of his cosy, spoilt-brat, middle-class life, out of his Boys' Own adventure: only two years ago, a few streets away from where Jamie and Swifty had found the money, a small boy on a bike had got in the way of gun-runners and had been shot dead . . .

She looked at Swifty's white, frightened face and she was filled with dread.

Tom was looking bewildered. He hadn't grasped the implications . . .

She put a smile on her face and said to Swifty: 'Now don't worry, we'll look after you,' but she didn't feel anything like as confident as she sounded.

'You're not going to the police, are you?' Swifty cried, afraid of what that might mean for him.

She thought a moment. She had a horrible feeling that in any case going to the police was not the answer. She'd heard too much from her ex-husband about gang revenge on those who get involved and then inform to the police . . .

Swifty was waiting anxiously for her answer. 'I might not have to . . .' She smiled as reassuringly as she could manage. 'Leave it to me.'

But that night she didn't sleep any better than Swifty did.

After arriving on B1, she went to see Dan as soon as she had a moment free.

He was sitting on his bed with his earphones on. He looked up and saw her, and looked away again quickly, hoping she wasn't really bearing down on him. The last thing he needed was another run-in with her. She'd already had her say; did she want to grind his nose in it?

She was at his side. Slowly, reluctantly, he took the earphones off.

'I want a word with you, Dan.'

He clung to the remnants of his aggression. 'Yeah?'

She was unperturbed. 'In private.'

She turned and walked away to the office, and he had no option but to follow.

Calmly she held the door open and showed him in.

'What's all this about?' he demanded irritably. 'I told you there won't be no more trouble.'

'I know . . .'

He said quickly: 'If it's about your car, I'm sorry I broke into it, right? It was Swifty's fault –'

She cut him off and said, to his surprise: 'It's not about the car. Sean's explained about that.'

'Well what, then?'

'I want to talk to you about Simmo.'

He gave a sharp snort of warning and alarm. 'I'm not getting mixed up in anything to do with Simmo. He's bad news.'

Sandra's heart flipped as she heard this confirmation of her fears, but she kept to her purpose. She narrowed her eyes. 'Then I might have to speak to the police about my car.'

He clenched his fists. She was too much of a match for him.

She asked coolly, 'How well do you know him . . . and that woman, his mother?'

'Who?'

'She came to see him – she was here the day he discharged himself.'

He laughed and told her what by now she was expecting to hear: 'That wasn't his mother!'

'Who was it, then?' She was anxious to know; and he felt suddenly at an advantage again.

'Why should I tell you?' he asked, surly once more.

She sighed. 'Look, Dan – all this hitting out. You can't fool me, I know it's just a front.' She became more serious, and now she was talking to him properly, sincerely. 'I'm worried about Sean. He can't look after himself like you can. He's only a little boy, and he's in over his head and very frightened. I need you to help me – you're the only person who can.'

She was looking at him straight, no patronizing, no wheedling or manipulating; just one adult talking frankly to another.

He warned her, frankly, seriously: 'Don't mess with Cath Wilson.'

'Is she involved in some kind of drug dealing?'

He shook his head. 'She lends money.'

She let out a breath. It wasn't as bad as she'd feared, but it was still pretty serious.

Dan went on: 'She charges interest. A *lot* of it. And if you get behind with your payments, you end up in here.' Cath Wilson did have her minders and thugs to do some very nasty work for her.

'Where does Simmo fit in?'

'He's her runner.'

She made a decision. 'I need her address.'

He shook his head in genuine ignorance. 'She just lives on the estate, that's all I know. There'll be loads, though, that do know, those that owe her. You'd only have to ask around.'

'Dan.' She was smiling suddenly, warmly. 'You know, I really appreciate this.'

And he nodded that she was welcome and grinned back.

Martin was redoing the corridor wall, painting out Dan's graffiti. In the ward kitchen near by, Mags handed Keely a congratulations card for passing her exams. It was a joke card, and they were laughing their heads off at it when Rob stepped in.

All three froze in awkwardness. 'Sorry, Keely,' said Rob stiffly, 'I didn't have time to get you a card.' He was about to step out again when he remembered. 'Congratulations,' he said, also stiffly, and was gone.

They felt terrible.

He was taking it really badly.

*

Rob went off to feed Jude. The job of nursing Jude was an especially skilled one, and Sandra Mitchell had appointed Rob to carry it out, even if he hadn't passed his exams.

This morning he tried to encourage Jude to feed himself. 'That's right,' he urged patiently, as Jude reached out awkwardly with his right hand for the spoon. 'No . . .' Rob warned gently, as Jude tried to use his left hand as well. 'Never mind,' he added calmly, as Jude's left hand knocked the spoon out of his right.

They made some progress, and Rob was in a better mood by the time he went to make a bed with Keely. She began to think he might be getting over his disappointment quite quickly, after all.

They stopped at Ellie's bed. Ellie had been bright earlier, squealing as she played with Heather and Debbie, but now she was tucked up between the sheets, looking pale. 'What's the matter, Ellie?' Keely asked.

'My tummy still hurts.'

Keely put her hand on the little girl's brow. 'Head ache?'

'A bit.'

And only yesterday they'd decided there was nothing wrong and they could send her home.

'I don't know,' Keely smiled reassuringly. 'What are we going to do with you?'

As they moved away from the bed Rob said, 'Something's obviously upsetting her.'

Keely frowned. 'But her parents come and see her regularly, and they seem all right.'

'Could be an act. For our benefit.' He felt she wasn't listening, discounting his opinion. After all, he thought bitterly, it was only the opinion of an unqualified nurse . . .

She didn't see that he was bristling. She was thinking: 'Though I *have* noticed that her mum has come alone the last few times. Her dad hasn't been there . . .'

She said: 'Perhaps I'd better have a word with Dr Gallagher. What do you think?'

He said stiffly, his voice full of meaning: 'You don't need my advice, do you?'

And once again she felt bad.

The two nurses had another run-in later. An appendectomy patient was coming up from Theatre, and Keely asked Rob to deal with her.

He stopped, his shoulders set in controlled irritation. 'I'm quite busy at the moment, with Jude.'

'Oh . . .' she said, growing awkward and trying to make amends. 'Well, after you've finished.'

He gave the impression of counting to ten, then said with exaggerated patience: 'If Jude's going to improve, he needs constant attention. You know the kind of care he'd get on a neuro ward.'

Now Keely was a little sharp. 'But we're not a neuro ward, are we? There are other patients.'

'And there are other nurses,' he said coldly.

Keely was upset. She had to make a conscious effort to hold down her feelings as she turned to little Heather. Heather was crying pitifully. She had lost her panda; she had looked everywhere, but it was nowhere to be found.

Yet again, something had gone missing. And none of the other missing items had been found . . .

Ellie brought her a fluffy elephant from the array on top of her own locker. 'Here you are, Heather,' she said kindly, 'you can borrow this.' And at last Heather was consoled.

Keely noticed that, despite her busy, motherly manner, Ellie was still looking pale . . .

As soon as Kieran arrived for his round, she did what she'd been planning to do and had a word with him about Ellie. 'She doesn't seem to be recovering after all.'

By now Kieran was pretty certain of his diagnosis, that Ellie was suffering abdominal migraine. It all fitted: the stomach ache, the headaches, the fact that Ellie sometimes complained of not being able to see properly – but then would recover and be as right as rain.

Keely suggested, 'Do you think there might be trouble at home?' She told him of her suspicions, and her observation that Ellie's dad had not been around lately.

Kieran considered the possibility and nodded thoughtfully. Abdominal migraine was often stress-related . . .

When they announced to Ellie their decision not to send her home after all, she looked happier, they noted, and she snuggled into her duvet, cosily wiggling her feet. No doubt about it, something was making her more glad to be in hospital than at home . . .

Not long afterwards Diane and Keely looked across and saw that her mother had arrived, once again without her dad. Settling a patient near by, they heard Ellie say tearfully, 'Why can't Dad come?'

Her mother replied, 'I know it's hard for you, love, but he had to go. We're doing what we think's best for you.'

Keely and Diane exchanged significant glances. It did look as though Keely's hunch was right.

Not long into the morning, Sandra Mitchell arranged for someone to cover for her; then she went out through the hospital doors and made for her car.

She didn't tell anyone where she was going.

Ten minutes later, she was drawing up on the newer side of Middleton Estate. Dan had been right: she only had to wind down her window and make an inquiry of a passer-by to get what she needed to. Cath was clearly a well-known figure in the area. The woman Sandra was questioning indicated a row of neat, two-storey maisonette flats with lacy curtains and frilly blinds at their windows. Halfway along, she pointed out the windows of one particular first-floor flat, protected by elaborate wrought-iron bars. On the wall beside them gleamed an ostentatiously large burglar-alarm. This was Cath's flat.

Sandra didn't feel nearly as brave as Sean was trustingly expecting her to be on his behalf. So this was the lot of parents, she thought, grimly: to be brave and fierce when you didn't feel it, to put aside your own fears for the sake of another, dependent and helpless. She thought of Swifty's frightened face, and she did suddenly feel fierce, fierce and angry that he should be threatened.

She got out of the car.

Her pulse was banging, nevertheless, as she made for the flats' entrance.

At the turn in the stair she realized that someone else was already there before her at the door of Cath's first-floor flat.

She drew back, but not before she had seen this sight: a young woman with two small children, handing over money. The door slammed shut and the woman trailed her children down the stairs.

Sandra stood back to let them pass. The children were whining and ill-looking, and the grey face of the thin young woman was set in an expression of utter resignation. So abandoned was she to her situation that she hardly noticed Sandra on the stairs as she passed.

Sandra went on up, towards the door of the woman who held the power to condemn people to such misery . . .

She knocked on the door.

There was a silence and then footsteps, and then the door opened.

'So. It's you.' Cath didn't look friendly at all.

'I've got the money for you.'

Cath nodded her head as if to say that this was only to be expected, in view of what would have happened if she hadn't . . . She said sharply, 'You'd better come in.'

Sandra hesitated, but then she stepped inside.

She followed Cath into her plush but flashy living room. She looked around, listening out. To her relief, there didn't seem to be anyone else in the flat.

Cath stood waiting, and Sandra opened her bag and took out the packet.

Cath snatched it, the sharp rattle of her metal bracelets making Sandra flinch. Cath looked at the parcel, ripped and coming apart, and sneered her suspicion.

'It's all there, I can assure you,' Sandra told her.

Tom had replaced the hundred pounds that Swifty and Jamie had spent. Swifty had stood and watched him counting it out, his face contorted with regret. For the first time in his short, cushioned life, he had found it painful to see his dad hand out money for him.

Cath glittered a threat. 'So you say. Listen, lady, I don't take anyone's word for anything. People pull all kinda strokes.'

And she sat and counted it.

When she got to the end, Sandra nodded in confirmation and relief and made ready to go.

Cath stood up in threat and mock disbelief. 'You don't think this settles it, do you?'

Sandra was afraid.

The woman came up to her and put her face close. 'I charge interest. Didn't anyone tell you?'

Sandra kept her voice steady. 'That money wasn't a loan.'

'No. It was *stolen*.'

Sandra stepped back and asked significantly: 'Have you reported the theft to the police?'

It was a vain threat.

The other hissed: 'What I do is legal. Those two kids nicked this money from Simmo.'

'Those two children had no idea what they were getting into.'

'Is that supposed to be an excuse?'

'It's the truth.'

Cath gave a scornful laugh but then grew deadly serious. 'Listen, lady, I provide a service. There aren't many caring bank managers round here, so people come to me. If it wasn't for me, people'd starve. They wouldn't know where their next penny was coming from. You don't know what it's like.' She paused. 'And I've got a reputation. Thing is, see, if they think I'm a soft touch, they'll try it on. First they'll be a day late with their payment. Then two days. Then, next thing, they've legged it.' She narrowed her eyes meaningfully. 'So you see, anyone who crosses me has to know they can't get away with it.'

Sandra swelled with anger. 'I'm warning you, if anything happens to those two boys –'

Cath gave a nasty crack of laughter. '*You're* warning *me*?'

Sandra finally snapped. 'Yes, *Ms* Wilson, I'm warning *you*! I'm no soft touch, either! Don't go telling me you're providing a service, unless it's for yourself!' She gave an angry gesture, indicating the furniture-stuffed room. 'Don't go telling me you're doing anyone any favours. You know, if I could, I'd have given that money back to the people you've exploited. Instead of which, I have *returned your lost property. Intact*.' She stressed the last words carefully and returned Cath's gaze levelly. 'And such a favour does not deserve to be greeted with the kind of threat I believe you have just made. Which threat,' she added with deliberate lightness, '*does* constitute a serious criminal offence.'

And Cath stood back, surprised and defeated, as Sandra turned and made her exit.

It was lunch-time by the time she got back to the hospital. Tom and Swifty were waiting anxiously, with Jamie in tow.

She smiled. 'Well, Sean, you won't need to go to the police and confess to them about taking the money.' They stared at her with growing relief. 'And I don't think you'll be hearing from Simmo or Cath Wilson again.'

Swifty didn't care, even in front of Jamie: full of gratitude and joy, he flung himself into Sandra's arms.

You couldn't knock it really, having a dragon on your side.

Kieran told Mrs Latimer when she came in: 'I've decided to tell Jude what happened to Phil.'

'But will he understand?'

'We don't know. But if he does, well, Phil was his friend. He has a right to be told.'

But Mrs Latimer was horrified. If he did understand, what would it do to him, when he was already so distressed?

After the way the Latimers had handled Leanne,

Kieran had expected this. He explained: 'It may sound cruel, but we want to provoke a response.'

Finally she agreed to it, and they wheeled Jude into the quiet of the empty Day Room and sat, one on each side of him.

Mrs Latimer began: 'Dr Gallagher's got something to tell you, Jude.'

Jude stared at the ceiling, giving no response.

Kieran leaned forward to attract his attention, and Jude swivelled his eyes towards him. 'You've been in a car crash. You were in a car with some of your friends. Do you remember?'

Jude gazed at Kieran vaguely.

'Do you remember their names? There was Sarah. And Dan.'

Jude seemed to be surveying the shape of Kieran's chin.

'And Phil.'

Jude leaned a little closer, intent, it seemed, on Kieran's stubble.

'You were all hurt. Sarah and Dan are in hospital here with you. They're both getting better.'

Mrs Latimer started to cry quietly at Jude's lack of a proper response, and Jude's gaze shifted with seemingly dispassionate interest to the sound.

'But, Jude, Phil wasn't so lucky. We thought he was going to be all right. But he died.'

Jude's gaze shifted back around to Kieran, just as blank.

'Phil's dead, Jude.'

Jude caught sight of a shaft of sunlight on the ceiling and stared at it with interest.

Mrs Latimer went on crying.

When she'd recovered, she took something out of her bag and showed it to Kieran. It was her own idea for stimulating Jude, a home video he'd taken himself.

'Good idea,' Kieran smiled, touching her arm and leaving Rob to supervise.

Rob set up the VCR machine. Leanne came in from the main ward, and she, Rob and Mrs Latimer settled down with Jude to watch.

Jude gazed at the flashing screen as the tape began winding before the start of the film. Mrs Latimer talked gently to him: 'We're going to show you a video, Jude. You're on it. And your friends. Leanne's on it, too.'

Quietly Sarah entered the Day Room and sat down on the floor and began to watch, behind the others.

The film started. On the screen appeared a wobbly close-up of a birthday cake with nine candles, and written on it: HAPPY BIRTHDAY LEANNE. Jude's eyes, though expressionless, were fixed on the silent screen, and Mrs Latimer talked him through it. 'This is Leanne's ninth birthday. Do you remember, Jude? I made that chocolate cake.

There's you, look, lighting the candles.' Into the frame came the old Jude, and the camera pulled back on him, gangling, grinning, lighting the candles and making a joke so that everyone on screen at the party laughed. Jude the joker. He snuffed the match, and Leanne blew all the candles out in one go.

Behind them in the Day Room, Dan came and leant in the doorway and, unnoticed by the rest of them, began watching too.

At that moment Faye hit the main ward. She had come back again after all. She was ready for action and in no mood to have anyone get in her way. She pushed Boz's trolley aside, causing him to splutter that he'd report her. Seeing where Dan was, she made a beeline for the Day Room door.

She went up behind Dan and tickled him.

Mrs Latimer was saying: 'And there's Faye.'

Faye realized what was happening. Her eyes swung to the screen and her skin prickled with shock at the sight of herself and Jude standing posing in the park, arms slung round each other, a fag dangling from Jude's grinning mouth. On screen behind them, the gang was playing football in the tennis courts. The football hit Jude on the back of the head. His poor head, which had now been so damaged . . . But the on-screen Jude was unhurt: the ball bounced off again, and he swirled about in mock anger and went chasing after the culprit: Phil.

Faye couldn't bear it. She grabbed Dan's hand,

mouthing, 'Come on,' and led him out of the Day Room.

On the film, the camera wobbled its way to a corner of the tennis courts and hounded down a couple snogging: Sarah and Dan. They broke off, giggling; Sarah hid her head and Dan put two fingers up at the camera, and the camera wobbled more as the person holding the camera laughed.

Watching in the Day Room, Sarah cringed inwardly, full of confused feelings of sadness and shame.

Rob and Mrs Latimer were watching Jude's face. Throughout, he had stared at the screen impassively. Not a flicker of recognition, not a flicker of emotion.

The film wound on: now the old Jude had caught Phil and was dragging him towards the camera, Phil's head tucked under his arm. Phil was protesting in mock melodramatic terror and Jude, ever grinning, was pretending to threaten to punch his head underarm-style. His head . . .

Mrs Latimer wanted to look away. But she said: 'What are you doing to that poor boy, Phil? He's such a rascal . . .' She corrected herself. 'Was.'

And as the on-screen Jude was pulled away for a snog by Faye, leaving the rascally Phil to cavort for the camera, a single tear tracked its way down the impassive, watching face of Jude in the Day Room.

What did it mean? Did it mean that he understood what had happened to Phil? They couldn't tell.

Under the stairs in the corridor, it was Faye and Dan who were snogging now.

Faye came up for air and said, 'We're off to Morecambe. Me and Lenny and Froggy. Come on.'

A figure in uniform appeared beside them. '*What's* going on!!?' It was Nurse Keely Johnson.

'What's it look like?' Faye asked her insolently.

'Well, you can just pack it in!'

'Jealous?' Faye sneered and laughed. She got hold of Dan's hand. 'Come on, let's get out of here to Morecambe.'

Keely planted herself in their way. 'Dan's not going anywhere.' She turned to Dan. 'You've got physio, Dan.'

Faye stepped up to her. 'You mind your own business. This is nothing to do with you.' She was so close that Keely could smell her bubble gum.

'Oh yes it has.'

'He's fit enough. You're fit, aren't you, Dan?'

''Course I am,' Dan agreed, surly enough now he had a woman to back him up. 'I don't need no stinking physio.'

Keely took a step towards Faye in the way the girl had done to her. 'He doesn't have any choice. And any more nonsense from *you*, and you won't be allowed back on the ward.'

There was silence. She stood her ground and waited. Faye waited. They glared at him, both of them. Dan looked from one to the other, then he shrugged at Faye, as if to say it was out of his hands.

Faye looked at them both contemptuously. 'Say goodbye to Jude for me,' she said nastily, walking off.

Keely felt a bit shaken as she walked back to the ward with a sullen Dan. She felt she'd only just won, and then only by sinking to Faye's level, acting like a scrapping teenager. She sighed. All those policies of talking to the patients, getting them to understand; sometimes it seemed they didn't get you anywhere. It was just a question of who could out-glare whom, and who could shout whom down . . .

Debbie was going home today.

Sarah hung round her bed, helping her to get packed. She was dreading Debbie's going. It would mean no more visits from Tim . . .

'It must be nice having a brother like Tim,' she said, passing Debbie her get-well cards.

Debbie grinned knowingly. 'Is it true, what Dan wrote on the wall?'

'No!' Sarah cried in horror. And she wandered off, and went and sat miserably on her own bed.

Keely, passing, noticed that she was in the

doldrums and guessed what was up. 'Fed up about Debbie going home?'

Sarah nodded.

Keely sat down, grinning. 'Tim?'

Sarah saw it was no good pretending. 'I can't even look him in the face after what Dan did.'

'Oh, come on!' Keely cried. 'You're not going to let Dan dictate your life, are you?'

'Well, I don't know what Tim thinks . . .' It must have made her seem so silly. If she'd ever had any chance with him, that had probably ruined it for good.

'Listen, Sarah. Boys don't always find it easy to talk about their feelings. They can be shy. And proud.'

Sarah looked at the nurse doubtfully, hopefully. 'Do you think that's it?'

Keely nodded, seeing the growing confidence in Sarah's face.

She moved away again, pleased to have proved herself wrong about not being able to talk these kids out of their problems.

When Tim arrived to collect Debbie, Sarah asked him to come and talk to her in the Day Room, but he didn't react in the way that her chat with Keely had led her to expect. He seemed suspicious, on edge.

She plucked up her courage, though. She said,

straight out: 'I'd like to see you again. Will you come out with me when I get home? We could go for a burger . . .'

He was looking at the floor. 'I can't.'

'Why not? Have you got a girlfriend?' This was what she'd been dreading most to hear.

He shook his head. 'No one special.'

She asked in amazement, 'Then why not? We get on really well together, don't we?'

He nodded miserably.

'Then why?' She added, bravely, to help him out, if he *was* just scared of showing his feelings: 'I really like you.'

He looked up at her, straight at her. 'I like you too.' But there was such a sad look in his eyes.

She was starting to feel vaguely afraid. 'Then why not?'

'I can't. Because of what you did.'

It was as though she had been hit in the stomach. 'But I'm *sorry* for what I did! You *know* I am! I'm going to change!' She could feel herself starting to cry.

He was gentle, but insistent. 'Yes, I know. But I just can't forget what you've done.'

'Tim – please . . .'

'I'm sorry.' He touched her arm. Then: 'I'd better get Debbie. Goodbye, Sarah.'

And he had gone.

*

Jude was making progress with his motor skills: at lunch-time he had managed to lift a beaker to his mouth and drink by himself.

'And he cried this morning,' Mrs Latimer said, with hope in her face.

Kieran knew it would be a mistake to let her hopes rise too high. He said: 'Well, a tear fell from his eye. That's all we can really say. It *could* have been because of what he heard and saw, or it could have simply been irritation caused by the flickering of the screen.'

Mrs Latimer looked downcast.

Later, Leanne sat down in front of him but she found herself unable to talk to his staring face.

Rob encouraged her: 'Talk about home. Any pets?'

She thought. 'We've got a cat . . .' and she began to tell Rob a tale of the cat's misdeeds.

He interrupted her. 'Don't tell me, tell Jude.'

So, uncertainly, awkwardly, she began telling Jude. Idly he watched her moving mouth. But as she got into the tale, she forgot to be awkward. 'On Sunday, Mr Jackson – you know, from next door – went out and left his Sunday dinner on the kitchen table. He was only gone a few minutes, but when he came back he saw Tigger jumping out of the window, and the chicken was all over the floor! Tigger had eaten most of it.' She laughed and looked up. Jude was grinning a slow, lopsided grin.

'Did he think it was funny?' Leanne asked Dr Gallagher.

'He might have. We can't really say.'

Then something happened which seemed to the family like a setback. While Leanne was still sitting with him, he suffered his first epileptic attack. His eyelids began to flutter and his head and arms to jerk. She screamed and jumped back, and stood in horror as the staff dealt with him calmly, turning him on to his side and administering injections and oxygen.

The attack was soon over, but the family was shaken. Jude had never had an epileptic attack before. A shattered Mrs Latimer said to Dr Gallagher: 'I thought he was starting to get better.'

Kieran assured her: 'In some ways, yes, he is. You must try not to get the epilepsy out of proportion. It's very common with injuries of this kind.'

'Will he have more?'

'Well, we can stabilize the condition to stop the attacks happening. But yes, he'll probably have them for the rest of his life.'

'As if he hadn't got enough to cope with.' Mrs Latimer sighed, her eyes brimming with tears.

Eight

It seemed to the staff that things were finally quietening down on the ward and that by next morning they could all settle down to an orderly routine.

It looked as though Faye had given up on her mates, and wouldn't be returning to cause trouble any more. And Sarah and Dan were keeping quiet and well out of each other's way.

Only Keely noticed that Sarah was so quiet that in fact she seemed depressed, in spite of their little chat yesterday.

Sarah was going by as Keely began the drugs round with Rob, and Keely hailed her anxiously. 'Sarah –' Sarah stopped reluctantly, and Keely asked nervously, 'Everything all right?'

'Waste of time.' Sarah was bitter, and clearly pained at having to make this admission.

Keely felt dreadful. She felt responsible. *She* had encouraged Sarah to speak to Tim, *she* had pushed her into what now turned out to be her humiliation. 'Well,' she said desperately, 'at least you'll be going home tomorrow. Be back with your friends. And your family. That's what matters.'

Sarah turned on her eyes that were burning with anger and pain. Her *friends*? That lot that she should never have got mixed up with in the first place, who'd kill a person and think so little about it that they'd go and do the same thing all over again; who'd stab her in the back the minute it was turned? And her *family*? Her parents: so bound up in their own squabbles that they hardly had time for her, even now, when all this had happened? Going home was exactly what she dreaded: the neighbours against her for what she'd done, and her official interview with the police looming . . .

She glared at Keely. What did this nurse know about *any* of it? Dead easy for someone like her, with her cushy job and her cushy life, doling out the easy advice along with the drugs. She should never have listened to her.

'Just leave me alone,' she said bitterly, and turned away.

Keely watched her in dismay. She turned back to find Rob's white eyes regarding her coldly out of his dark face. 'You handled that well,' he said quietly, nastily.

Keely went cold. Rob was being terrible. And they'd always been such good mates . . . He was hardly speaking to her now, and he hadn't smiled at her once since the exam results had come out.

The drugs trolley business must have really rubbed his nose in it, though. They'd been so short-staffed yesterday – with Sandra Mitchell disappearing on her mystery outing – that, regardless of Rob's feelings, Keely had been promoted to take charge of the trolley on the drugs round. Rob, as the unqualified nurse not allowed to remain alone with the drugs, had to run around dispensing them to the patients, while she, the qualified nurse, stood by in charge of the prescriptions and the key.

Keely felt bad for Rob, but at the same time she was resentful that he should make such a determined effort to spoil her enjoyment of her own success.

Still, there was something happening today for Keely that made up for everything, that gave her a warm glow each time she thought of it as she worked: today was Lauren's third birthday, and last night Billy had rung from Southampton to say that unexpectedly he'd be making it home for her birthday tea. Keely had missed him so much, and Lauren was so excited at the thought of seeing him. Keely had flown to work this morning as though she'd had wings on her sensible heels. It would be just for one night, but for Lauren's birthday they'd be a proper family, together once again . . .

It was while she was thinking this that Martin,

the decorator, approached them at the trolley, passing on a message from the office. 'Keely, phone.'

'Don't mind me,' Rob told her, with an unmistakable note of insolence in his voice.

She turned to go, worried that the call might mean problems with Lauren, and he called her back quietly and significantly: 'Keely.' She looked back in inquiry, and he said quietly, 'Better not leave me here with the cabinet unlocked.'

She went red, and locked it quickly, resentful again at the way he was rubbing it in. Then she went off to answer the phone.

It was Billy. She knew straight away by the way he said her name that it wasn't good news. He couldn't come home after all. Another job had come up . . . He could make it at the weekend instead . . .

She heard the disappointment in his voice, but it did nothing to lessen the bitterness of her own. 'Oh, *Billy*! What am I going to say to Lauren? We were going to have a party. I've got cake and jelly . . .'

Qualified nurse she might be, but at that moment she was finding it hard to stop herself from crying.

And as she put the phone down miserably, Rob came sweeping into the corridor. He said with cold hostility: 'Are we going to do this drugs round, or aren't we? *I've* got other jobs to do, you know.'

She finally snapped. 'Just get off my back, will

you? It's not my fault you failed your rotten exams, so stop taking it out on me!'

All the while, Martin had been painting and quietly listening near by in the corridor. Now, as Keely strode back into the ward, he stopped work and watched her thoughtfully.

In the new peace that had settled in the ward, Kieran was doing his round, accompanied by Diane.

He examined Jude. 'Thanks, Jude,' he said when he'd finished. As usual Jude gave no response. It was now Kieran's opinion that they had done everything that could be done for him here on the ward. All that was needed now was for the result of Jude's neurological assessment to confirm this, and plans could be made to move him to a Rehabilitation Unit. Although it was too soon to make predictions, the likelihood was that Jude would never make a complete recovery and that he would require a lot of special care for the rest of his life. The only real job left for Kieran now was preparing Jude's family for this difficult reality.

He left Jude and moved on to Heather.

Listened in on by a nosy, gum-chewing Mel, he explained carefully to Heather that the surgeon would be taking away her mole and then patching up the place where it had been with a piece of skin taken from her thigh.

'Will it hurt?' Heather asked anxiously.

'It won't hurt at all. Might be a little bit sore afterwards.'

She smiled with relief, and he patted her head, then turned to Mel. Her tattoo was healing, and in a couple of days, he told her, she'd be able to go home.

She looked significantly at the two of them, Diane and Kieran, and commented: 'I think it's dead romantic. You two, together every minute of the day.'

Diane said wryly, 'We're just doing our jobs.'

Mel asked her: 'Does he ever chat up other women, to make you jealous?' Neither noticed the edge of seriousness in her tone, and they rolled their eyes and good-naturedly changed the subject, then moved on. Neither picked up the hint that there was more trouble brewing between patients on the ward.

The trouble was this: at breakfast-time, Mel had come to the table late after applying her make-up, to find Wiggy sitting next to Natalie, the twelve-year-old girl who'd just had her appendix out. As far as Mel was concerned, this Natalie was a Class One Bore: the type who wore pleated skirts and read books about ponies. Today, after her operation, she sat in her drippy dressing-gown, her face as white as a sheet – a real sight, in Mel's opinion. But there was Wiggy, *talking* to her! And not only that:

as Mel reached the table, Natalie was asking Wiggy if he'd like to play chess! *Chess*, of all things!

Intending to rescue him, Mel sat down on his other side.

He ignored her. He moved his elbow, cutting her out, and leant further towards Natalie. He told Natalie, yes, he'd like to.

Mel couldn't *believe* it! And there they were now, Wiggy and Natalie, moving chess-pieces towards each other at the centre table, and looking up at each other and smiling . . .

She sat, waiting for the chess game to finish, preparing to get Wiggy back to herself the moment it did.

She looked up from her magazine. They had finished the game. She looked again in horror. Natalie was twirling something on her finger . . . The eternity ring that Wiggy had bought for *her*, for Mel, and which he hadn't yet given her! As Natalie admired it on her own finger, Wiggy was looking on fondly, pleased with himself.

Mel was too upset to move as they got up from the table and shuffled out at Natalie's slow, post-operative pace towards the drinks machine.

'What's up?' Keely was at her side. Even as she asked the question, Keely sussed the situation.

Mel said grimly: 'I thought it was true love.'

Keely tried not to smile, thinking back to her own similar tribulations. She showed Mel the marks where her own tattoo had been done. 'Grimmy,' she read for her. 'Short for Andrew Grimshaw.' She grinned. 'I thought *that* was true love. He's horrible now, with a great big beer-gut.'

Mel didn't see the funny side. She said: 'She's got no right to take him off me. And I'm not going to let her.'

And she was up off the bed and gone.

At the drinks machine, Wiggy was handing Natalie a coffee. He looked up a bit uncertainly as Mel bore down on them, ready to do battle. 'Mel . . .'

'You've remembered who I am, then?' she challenged. She turned to Natalie, pointing triumphantly and possessively at Wiggy's bandage. 'You know what he did for me?'

'Yes,' replied Natalie calmly. 'Stephen's explained all that.'

Mel stared at him in disbelief. *Stephen?* That was his name, but it wasn't what he was *called*. Mel had never *thought* of him as *Stephen*.

Wiggy looked awkward, then gathered confidence. '*Wiggy*'s childish.'

Mel was devastated. It was *Wiggy* by which she knew him, it was from *Wiggy* that she had had a promise of eternal devotion, it was '*Wiggy*' she'd had permanently tattooed on her arm . . .

She made a lunge and grabbed Natalie's hair.

Natalie screamed, forced by the pain to bend the wrong way over her stomach wound, then she reached out and grabbed Mel's own hair and pulled hard –

'Melanie! Natalie!' The roaring voice was Keely's. She stood fuming like a sergeant-major. 'I think we've had quite enough fighting on this ward, don't you?'

So much for peace, thought Keely, and so much, once again, for calming patients down with a cosy little chat.

Kieran and Diane had moved on to Ellie. Today she was lying, curled up on her bed, looking miserable and pale and complaining of stomach ache and headache again. Diane told Kieran about the conversation she and Keely had overheard the previous day between Ellie and her mum.

Kieran instructed her: when Ellie's mum came in today, they would get her into the office and ask her a few straight questions.

They were surprised when they did. They had assumed a marital breakup: the truth had never occurred to them. Ellie's dad, it turned out, had had to move to Sheffield for work, and Ellie's illness and hospitalization had forced Ellie and her mum to stay on in Manchester in temporary accommodation.

It soon became clear why Ellie had fallen ill in the first place, and why the thought of leaving hospital always caused a relapse: she was terrified at the prospect of leaving her friends and the world she knew in Manchester, and moving to a different, possibly horrible place, a place where she'd know no one and be entirely alone . . .

Kieran explained to Mrs Barrett that it was the situation itself that was making Ellie ill, so prolonging the stay on B1 was no solution.

At first Mrs Barrett wasn't convinced. 'But you see how upset she gets each time she thinks she's going to be discharged! And then she's always ill again.'

But they had to break the cycle. The only way that Ellie could get better would be by facing up to the situation – moving to Sheffield and settling down as quickly as possible, and then getting over it. It was another case of having to be cruel to be kind.

'I'll discharge her tomorrow,' Kieran decided firmly.

Just then the door burst open. 'I want a skin graft!' a wild-faced Mel demanded.

'Mel, I'm talking –' Kieran protested, but she barged on.

'I heard you telling Heather about it.' She had ripped off her bandage and was pointing to her wobbly '*Wiggy*' tattoo. 'He's a cheating sneak! I want a skin graft. Now!'

As expected, Ellie was very upset when Diane told her the news.

'Why can't I stay here?' she sobbed.

'You'll soon get better. You'll make lots of new friends.'

After a while Ellie got up and went to her locker. She sniffed, 'Then I'd better give these back.'

Diane stared. Inside Ellie's locker were Heather's missing panda, Tanya's troll and Debbie's Travel Scrabble.

Ellie's face crumpled again. 'I'm sorry . . . I'm sorry . . .'

Diane gathered her in her arms. 'Don't worry. I'll sort it out. I'll get them back to the people they belong to.' She hugged her, understanding why Ellie had done it. About to lose everything, all her friends, Ellie had desperately needed to keep something belonging to these people who were befriending her at the moment, but whom she was going to lose as well . . .

There was another skirmish when Boz, the sweet-trolley man, locked horns with Dan again.

'Can of Coke,' Dan demanded surlily. Then he changed his mind: 'No, two.'

Boz challenged: 'Ever heard of a certain word beginning with P?'

'Prat?' Dan asked with mild insolence, at which Boz drew back the can he was about to hand over. 'I don't have to serve you, you know.'

Dan waited till he'd got the cans and paid for them,

then he retorted: 'And I don't have to smack you in the mouth, but I might.'

He walked away to Boz's cries: 'Hey, pal, you can't speak to me like that! I'll report you!'

It was the sight of Sarah sitting on her own at the table in the middle of the ward that had made Dan buy another can.

He took it over to her and handed it across.

She looked up at him, uncertain, half hostile. He nudged it in the air towards her, telling her go on, take it – and finally she did.

He was awkward. He asked, 'Anyone coming in to see you today?'

She mumbled, 'Only my mum.' It was only ever her mum, not her dad, not her friends, it was as though she'd lost everyone, now that this had happened . . . Then she asked: 'What about you?'

'Nobody.' No Faye.

After a moment she said, not without a hint of bitter triumph, 'Not very nice is it, being chucked?'

He said, suddenly earnest, 'It wasn't like *that*. We weren't *going out* . . . She was upset, about Jude. We all were . . . It was nothing.'

She looked hard at him. She was so desperate not to feel so alone . . . And she could see he meant it. Or he thought he did, at this moment. But how could she ever trust him again?

She looked down, not knowing how to react.

They both sat there with their heads bowed, tapping their cans and not knowing what to say next.

Dan said finally, 'I can't wait to get out of this place.'

Sarah suddenly felt disgusted. 'Oh, you're really looking forward to going to the police station, are you?'

And his reaction, full of bravado, disgusted her further: 'They won't do nothing. Tell us we've been naughty little children.'

'Then what?'

'Then we do what we want.'

'Like we used to?'

'Why not?'

She stared at him.

He was saying, 'What's wrong with having a laugh with your friends?'

She felt breathless with disbelief 'A *laugh*?' She pointed to Jude. 'Did you say a *laugh*?' She stared at him. 'You just don't get it, do you? It's not going to be like it was before. How *can* it be? After this?'

And she almost spat in exasperation as she got up and left her Coke half drunk.

It was as though there could never really be happy endings. As though the awful things that had happened, though they seemed to be over, were always there afterwards, simmering just beneath the surface.

Sandra Mitchell knew she'd never feel the same about letting Sean go around alone – she'd always be worrying about his safety, she'd always be dreading the worst. Just like any mother, she supposed, with a wry smile to herself.

When Sean had asked this morning if he could go fishing that evening with Jamie down the canal, she had felt instantly alarmed. But she had kept her fears to herself and instead had said brightly, 'I thought you were washing your father's car tonight towards paying off your hundred-pound debt.'

And that had settled it.

Or so she thought.

At half-three that afternoon, Swifty came running into the hospital with his hand bound and bleeding, followed by a panicking Jamie.

'But what'll she *say*?' cried Jamie. 'She'll know you were bunking off school!'

'Yeah, but I need a nurse!' Swifty was gasping, his face white.

Jamie waited in the foyer, so he didn't witness Swifty burst into the office, for all the world a little boy desperate for motherly comfort.

The moment Sandra saw the bleeding rag, her heart turned over. 'What have you *done*?'

And when she saw what it was – not an injury inflicted by thugs, but a wound from a fish-hook – in relief she forgave him everything, including bunking off school.

Jamie came into the office and saw Mitchell the dragon bending solicitously over Swifty, and Swifty the supposed hard man lapping up her attentions. He scratched his head. What had come over them both?

Keely left early for Lauren's birthday with a far heavier heart than she'd expected to have.

Lauren was going to be so disappointed when Keely told her that Billy wasn't coming. And it would take a great effort for Keely to overcome her own sad feelings and drum up the birthday atmosphere Lauren deserved.

She got on the bus, and thought back to the day Lauren was born. Billy had been there, seventeen years old and overcome with emotion. He had been desperate to be in on it. It was Billy who'd been desperate for them to be together and be a proper family, in spite of her doubts . . . And in spite of her doubts they had, they had been a proper family in the end. Until things got too tough money-wise, and he had to go away for work. That was when she knew she really loved him, when she discovered how much she missed him.

Tonight, though, she couldn't help feeling that little nodule of resentment again: if he was really so keen to make a proper family, why didn't he try harder to get work near by instead? And of course, as usual, here she was, left holding the fort, looking after Lauren on her own, just as she would have been if she'd not relied on him in the first place.

And she couldn't suppress a resentful suspicion that, if he'd really wanted, he *could* have turned this job down tonight.

She got off the bus and put on a happy face for Lauren.

They had got to the cake and Lauren was just blowing out the candles, when the doorbell rang.

Keely jumped up with joy, but even as she got halfway to the door, she knew it couldn't be Billy, he'd have his key.

It was Martin, the decorator, holding a present for Lauren in one hand and a bunch of flowers in the other.

After she'd put Lauren to bed, she came and sat down, accepting the mug of coffee he'd made. She grinned. He'd made the difference to their party, and he'd been very good with Lauren. She was glad he'd turned up.

They were suddenly quiet though, now that Lauren was no longer their focus of attention. They had run out of things to say. Keely remembered that he'd brought her flowers, and she eyed them in their vase; she was beginning to feel a little awkward.

He said suddenly, seriously: 'I think you're doing a great job, Keely – looking after Lauren, working at the hospital, passing your exams . . .'

She gave a dismissive laugh. 'I just get on with things. Not much choice – I have to.'

He was gazing at her intently. 'People appreciate you. I can see it.'

She thought: But does Billy? And does he realize what I have to sacrifice . . .? She said, continuing her thoughts out loud, 'I just wish I could do something for *me* for once. Everything I do's for someone else. A lot of girls my age, they've got no responsibilities, they do what they like, go out when they like –' She broke off, realizing how she must sound. She said quickly: 'I wouldn't change what I've got, honest.'

He said, 'Let me take you out. Tomorrow, for a pizza.'

She replied suddenly, surprising herself, 'OK.'

Back at the ward, it was time for bed for the little ones. Someone was crying. It was Ellie, crying under her blankets, because tomorrow she'd have to leave the hospital and go to Sheffield. And because of what people would think of her taking those things. As soon as they were given back to their owners, all would be clear. What would Heather think?

Someone tweaked her blankets off her head; it was Heather. Ellie turned away in shame. 'There,' Heather said comfortingly, and Ellie felt something tucked into bed with her. It was the elephant she'd lent Heather to make up for the missing panda . . .

Her shame deepened, and her tears redoubled.

Earlier that evening, just before the shops closed, an old woman had looked round her dusty living room; then she had shut her door and gone out. Winnie was too old and frail now to keep up with the housework, but shopping she could still manage. She set off, shuffling towards the row of shops near by.

When she emerged from them, she was not unobserved. Someone was watching her: an unkempt, grey-faced youth with beaded hair. A scruffy dog at the lad's side made a sudden move towards her, and the youth restrained it with his hand.

Winnie set off back home. The youth waited some moments, then, after looking around carefully to check that no one was observing him, he began to follow.

Winnie had only been in one minute when the doorbell rang.

She opened the door. The lad was leaning against the doorframe, the dog alert at his side.

'Matt!' she cried in joy. 'Come in!'

Her delight was short-lived. She could see that the boy was ill. There were sores on his face. He sagged against the doorpost. As he tried to move, he began coughing, a dreadful fit of it that lasted until she had got him sitting down.

She surveyed him half sternly, half in fond forgiveness. 'What's happened this time?'

He stared back at her wearily, fifteen years old and with the eyes of an old man. She thought: 'Just a youth and with enough misery behind him to last a lifetime.' All his life he had been in care, mainly with foster parents, none of whom he'd ever got on with. He was always running off and sleeping rough. That was how she'd come across him the first time, almost tripping over him as he sat outside the supermarket, tucked up with the stray dog who'd befriended him.

She bent down now and rubbed the dog's back. 'How are you, Meff?' And Meff squatted hopefully, eyes shining, in expectation of the food she would surely give him.

She went off to the kitchen to open a tin of dog meat and one of tomato soup for Matt.

As she went, the youth, reviving now, looked round the room. He noticed the dust. Winnie was obviously coping less well now. She must be weaker and more vulnerable . . .

'Your foster parents will be worried,' she told Matt as she put the bowl of soup in front of him. She knew he hadn't told them about her: she was his refuge when he couldn't stand any more.

He said nothing, so she knew it must be bad between them this time. He coughed again, a great hacking cough that seemed as if it would rend him in two. She frowned. There was something about that cough, something she recognized of old . . . She went to get some cough linctus.

Two hours later, the cough was getting worse. An ache of worry was gnawing in her own chest. He slumped weakly in the chair, dozing fitfully. A certainty had been growing in her, and finally, in spite of what she knew he would say, she announced: 'I'd better call a doctor.'

'No!' He was fierce despite his weakness. 'You know what would happen! They'd call the social, and then I'd get sent back.'

She bit her lip. 'Well, at least go and lie down, then.' And, as best she could, she helped him up to bed.

In the chair downstairs she fretted, listening to him still coughing.

She couldn't sit still. She climbed the stairs again and stood outside his door on the landing. Inside, he was coughing, and tossing and turning . . . Meff was whimpering.

She opened his door. Matt lay in a tumble of bedclothes, his eyes half open, glistening and delirious, his face covered in sweat. Meff sat up and met her eyes, confirming what she knew she must do.

Winnie got herself down the stairs and dialled 999.

Nine

Early next morning Kieran Gallagher was walking with Sandra Mitchell towards B1 when he told her about the fifteen-year-old boy who had been brought in, coughing and feverish, last night. 'I put him in isolation as soon as the X-rays came through. Suspected open pulmonary tuberculosis.' He shook his head. 'It's a growing problem with the homeless. And once upon a time we thought we'd stamped out TB once and for all. So much for progress, eh?'

They stood, thinking about it gravely. Then Sandra asked: 'So you think he *is* homeless? There's no family? No address?'

Kieran shook his head. 'Just the old girl who came in with him – and she didn't seem to know him. Just called the ambulance. He must have been living rough for ages, the state of him.'

Sandra became businesslike and made to move to the office. 'Well, I'll get on to Social Services then.'

Kieran stopped her. 'There's no rush if you're busy, he won't be leaving here very fast. If it is TB he's going to be with us for a while. I've put him on triple therapy while we do some more tests.'

Which was how the truth about Matt and Winnie was not uncovered for the moment.

They hadn't noticed Winnie hanging back a little way along the corridor, and she was keeping too far away to hear what they were saying. With relief she watched them move on and waited for someone less dangerously official-looking to pass by. Mags, in her brown auxiliary uniform and with her homely, down-to-earth manner, came along, and Winnie moved towards her hopefully.

Mags surveyed her: a bedraggled, frail old woman, clutching fruit and looking uncertain. 'Are you lost, love?' she asked with brisk kindness.

Winnie whispered eagerly and confidentially, 'I'm looking for Matt.'

Mags knew nothing of Matt's admission, and she found the woman's secretive behaviour more than a little strange.

Winnie was whispering: 'I just want a minute with him. They said in Reception he'd been brought up here last night.'

Mags looked hard at her. As far as Mags knew, there was certainly no one called Matt on the Children's Ward this morning. The old woman was clearly doddery and confused. 'Let me ask Sister Mitchell –' and she made a move to get this awkward situation sorted out.

Winnie stopped her with an urgent hand on her arm. 'No, no, I only want to know how he is!'

Mags asked sceptically, 'Are you a relative?'

Winnie confirmed her suspicions by answering quickly, 'No!'

Poor Winnie: she had decided that if they thought she was a relative they'd start asking awkward questions. But in the next seconds she realized that by denying it she'd cut herself off from the right to see Matt.

And Sister Mitchell had appeared on the scene and was putting two and two together. 'Are you the lady who found him and came in with him last night?'

'What's he said?' Winnie asked, panicking.

Sister Mitchell frowned. 'What about?' she asked curiously.

Winnie changed the subject quickly. 'I've brought him a bit of fruit.'

Sister Mitchell's face broke into a kind smile as she came to the same conclusion as Mags about Winnie: just a harmless confused old woman. 'I'll see he gets it,' she said, smiling.

Winnie tried to take advantage of their view of her. 'Can't I see him?'

Sister Mitchell shook her head, gently patronizing. 'Not if you're not a relative. He's very ill. He's been put in isolation. It was a good job you brought him in when you did, and we're very grateful. But he's in good hands now.'

Winnie was devastated. 'Thank you,' she said vaguely. She stood still for a moment, then turned and wandered off as if in a daze. She was still clutching the fruit.

Mags called after her: 'Eh, don't you want to give it to us –?' But Winnie didn't turn around.

'Leave it,' said Sandra, shaking her head with cynical understanding.

Dan and Sarah were leaving today. But they wouldn't be going straight home, they were to be taken to the police station.

Sarah was petrified. She was watching the entrance with dread for the appearance of either of their parents.

'*I'm* not worried,' Dan told her. 'They can't touch us.'

He seemed so sure. But she couldn't believe it. How could they not be punished? The consequences of what they'd done were so terrible . . . She looked across at Jude, propped in his chair, clumsily pushing a toy car across his tray. She wanted to cry. What did that toy car mean to him? Did he have any memory of the real car that had done him so much damage?

Dan was saying, 'It's nothing. You just get warned. Cautioned, they call it.' It had happened to him before. 'Just do what they tell you. Don't look at them. And whatever you do, don't cry. They like it when you cry. They think they've got through to you. But they can't.' He grinned. 'We're under age – juveniles. They can't touch us. That's the joke.'

She looked across at Jude again. 'Some joke,' she thought sadly.

She said, 'I'm going to say goodbye to Jude. You coming?'

Dan looked across at Jude awkwardly, then he looked away again and didn't come.

Jude dropped the toy car and gazed at Sarah vaguely as she sat down beside him. 'I'm so scared, Jude,' she told him. It was not something she'd ever have dared tell the old Jude. 'Of everything. Of the police. Of going home. That's why I started hanging around with you lot in the first place – because I couldn't stand it, all the rows at home.'

For a moment he seemed to be looking at her intently, as though he understood every word she said. She wondered: did he? Who was she talking to? How much of the old Jude was left in there? What kind of person was it inside this big, baby-like shell? She had a sudden horrible feeling of disintegration – the whole world breaking up, breaking apart, everything spoilt.

Jude's attention had drifted. He was poking again at his toy car.

His attention was drawn to her once more as she stood up. Her mother had entered the ward, followed by Dan's dad. 'I've got to go.'

An unmistakable look of anxiety crossed Jude's face. He seemed to know what was happening, that they were leaving him.

She said: 'I'll come and see you. I promise. When I can.'

When she could . . . It would depend on what the police decided to do to her. They could send her away . . .

Jude watched as she walked towards her mother, who was picking up her packed case. His eyes slewed. Someone was standing beside him. Dan.

Dan looked at him awkwardly. It was the first time since the accident that he'd been able to bring himself to speak to Jude. What he said was: 'Ta-ra.'

Awkwardly, Dan stood there for another moment, then he turned away. Jude watched him the whole time. He watched, almost intently, as Sarah and Dan went with their parents out of the ward. For a few moments after they'd gone he sat staring almost sadly.

And then he turned his attention back to his toy car.

Sarah and her mother stepped up to the desk at the

police station. Behind them, Dan and his dad were already sitting on black plastic chairs. The room was stark, there was no one behind the desk. Sarah's mother rang the bell. They waited in the cold, blank atmosphere. Sarah looked back, but Dan was avoiding her eye.

Suddenly an inspector came out from a side door. He ignored Sarah and her mother, and said with blank sternness: 'Dan Miller?'

Dan and his dad stood up and the inspector held the door grimly and then shut it behind them as they passed in.

The desk sergeant appeared. Now it was Sarah's turn.

There was no smile from the female officer about to interrogate her. She pointed stiffly to where she wanted Sarah to sit.

Sarah sat down. She was trembling slightly. Her mother sat on a chair, a little behind her, also facing the interrogation desk.

The officer looked at her without expression. 'I'm Superintendent Chapman.'

She paused, noting Sarah's dread and horror at what was happening. She said significantly, 'You're very *lucky* to be here today, Sarah. For two reasons. One: you could have been dead. Which I'm sure you've thought about. Two: you could have been up in front of a juvenile tribunal, facing a very serious charge. And from which, given the evidence, you would have walked away with a criminal record.'

Sarah hung her head in horror, and the superintendent said sharply: 'Look at me when I'm talking to you.'

She looked up, hardly daring to meet the steely eyes of the officer. *Don't look at them,* Dan had said, and she knew why now: the way they looked at you filled you with such fear and shame. As if you were nothing. As if you were only fit for the worst. And she *was* nothing.

But the superintendent was saying: 'I know a lot about you, Sarah. I've talked to your teachers. They told me that you're not a bad person. They told me you're quite bright. But I had to question that. Because you had been party to stealing a car, which was then driven so recklessly that it killed one person, left another brain-damaged and seriously injured four others, including yourself.'

Sarah couldn't bear it, hearing these words she'd said already so many times to herself . . . 'I'm sorry,' she gasped.

The superintendent ignored this and asked pointedly, 'Why didn't you stop and think about the possible consequences?'

There was a silence. How could Sarah answer that, here, in this cold place, with these cold officials, and in front of her mother? How could she say it:

that she *had* thought about the consequences, that in fact she was scared stiff, that she was telling them to slow down? But that you didn't do that, not in that gang, and she was part of the gang, she had to be, it was the choice she had made, it was the way she had escaped from thinking about the misery of her home breaking up. It was a world where you could stop thinking about consequences or about anything, you just got hard and had a laugh.

She mumbled, 'I don't know.'

Superintendent Chapman sat back. 'Well, we're going to sit here until you've worked out exactly why you did it. Because if you don't know, then I've got no guarantee that you won't go back out there and do it all over again.'

Sarah saw then that she was going to have to convince them. She would have to say it anyway. She said, 'I knew it was wrong. I kept thinking whose car it might be. I was scared. The way Dan was driving . . .'

It came back to her: Dan grinning like a fiend, the skidding round corners, the archway spinning up . . . She said, 'I wanted to get out, I knew we were going to crash . . .' She remembered the girls' faces through the window and then the noise, and everything tumbling, and suddenly, something she hadn't remembered till now: her seat crushing into her, down on her, as it met the force of Jude's head . . .

She could hardly move when she had told it. She

felt collapsed, with grief and horror. She could hardly sit up in the chair.

Superintendent Chapman said unsympathetically, 'You chose to participate. You said you couldn't say anything. But you could. You had a choice. You say you knew it was wrong, yet you still chose to get in that car. You say you knew what was going to happen. But you didn't try and stop it.'

'I'm sorry,' she gasped.

The officer regarded her impassively. 'You behaved with gross irresponsibility.'

'I know.'

'Stand up.'

What was going to happen now?

The officer drew her shoulders back and made a formal announcement: 'If you are brought to my attention again in any subsequent criminal matter, I'll have no choice but to be considerably less lenient than I've been today. This is a caution. It's not a criminal record. But next time it will be. Do you understand?'

Sarah forced out her answer. 'Yes.'

A caution, as Dan had said it would be. But it wasn't nothing, as he'd said it would be. It was terrible, her whole world was splitting open, everything was leaking . . .

And she knew she would never be the same again.

*

Dan was shocked. He had expected another caution.

But the inspector was saying: 'Dan Graham Miller, you are charged that on September 19th 1994, in the county of Greater Manchester, without the consent of the owner or other lawful authority, you, Dan Graham Miller, took a mechanically propelled vehicle . . .'

It was one time too many, and this time the offence was too serious. This time he was being charged.

'. . . Owing to the driving of the vehicle an accident occurred by which injury was caused to persons, namely Jude Andrew Latimer . . .'

Now he would have a criminal record . . .

'. . . You are not obliged to say anything. But anything you do say may be taken down and used in evidence. Right, stand up.'

And they led him through and took his fingerprints and set him up for the photograph that would go on his criminal record.

The photographer snapped. In the split second before he did so, he noticed the boy's lip trembling.

Afterwards, when their parents had gone off to work, they sat side by side on a bench in the park.

Dan was subdued. He told Sarah: 'I've got to appear in court tomorrow morning, to be charged.'

She was crying softly. She couldn't stop thinking about Jude and Phil.

He put his arm round her tentatively. 'I'm sorry. About that stuff with Faye.'

She looked at him with sorrowful contempt. 'Is that supposed to make everything better? Nothing can make Jude better. He's going to be like that for the rest of his life. While we're growing up, he'll stay like that: a big baby. A zombie. Until he dies . . .' She began to sob. 'And Phil. For the rest of our lives he'll just be someone that died. When we were kids.'

'Don't keep thinking about them.' Dan shook his head as if to make them go away.

She threw his arm off. 'I can't *help* thinking of them! I'm not Faye! You're just as bad as her! *We* did that to them – hasn't it sunk in yet!!?'

He said helplessly, 'It was an *accident*!'

She stood up. 'It shouldn't have *happened*! We could have stopped it!'

He repeated defensively, 'It was an accident!'

She said no more to him. Filled with grief, she turned and left, ignoring the sound of him calling after her.

Halfway through the morning, Rob brought in a motorized wheelchair for Jude. He got the lad into it and began to teach him to use it. When Leanne arrived half an hour later, he had still not mastered the controls, but he was trying very hard.

'I'll help!' said Leanne, pleased with the whole idea.

She clambered up and sat in Jude's lap and began steering him around. It was great fun. She zipped this way and that, laughing.

After a while, she realized that Jude was waving his hand, trying to tell her something. It was the first time he'd tried to communicate with her. She was thrilled. She cried, 'What?' looking keenly in the direction his hand seemed to be jabbing. 'You want to go up the ward?' He kept jabbing in the same direction, and she decided that must be it, and so she turned the chair that way and set off.

Suddenly he grabbed her hand that was holding the controls and pulled it – and that was the moment she realized he'd been trying to say he wanted to work it himself. It was also the moment when the chair went out of control and careered straight for the sweet-trolley which Boz had just pushed on to the ward.

She screamed; people jumped out of the way; they crashed; Leanne went flying; sweets flew everywhere. Boz was yelling: 'You stupid little vandals, you want to be locked up, you belong in a zoo!'

And Jude was slumped across his strap, unable to sit himself up again. As if suddenly brought back to that other, horrific crash, he had an expression of terror on his face.

Rob propped him back up again, and Diane helped Leanne to her feet.

Leanne turned on Jude. 'You stupid idiot!' she

burst out, hysterical. Always crashing, he was all danger and smashing and spoiling things . . . She backed away from him, lolling in his chair, her own brother, broken and spoilt. 'You stupid, stupid idiot!' she screamed.

Winnie wandered round the hospital, looking for the place she dare not ask for. Then she saw the sign: ISOLATION UNIT. She followed the arrow.

She approached the door. A sign above the glass window read STRICTLY NO ADMITTANCE. Full of trepidation, she peered in. There was Matt, asleep and pale, attached to a drip. As she gazed, he seemed in his sleep to sense her there, and he stirred and opened his eyes. He gave her a look of eager relief. But, frightened by the sign, she signalled that she couldn't get to him, and he sank back, disappointed, and closed his eyes.

Miserably, she wandered away again.

Heather came rushing in gleefully to show something to Ellie. Her panda; she was waving it over her head. 'Look, Ellie, he's been found, Rob found him!'

Ellie turned away. So they hadn't told Heather the truth, then. But she still couldn't face her, she felt so ashamed.

Heather was puzzled that Ellie didn't want to share her good news. But then she was so miserable about going home today – or, rather, to Sheffield . . . They had tried hard all morning, staff and children, to persuade her that it wouldn't be so bad. But she couldn't be convinced.

When her mother arrived to collect her, she'd gone missing, and they had to set up a search for her.

Finally Mags found her, tucked away on the other side of the drinks machine. 'Come on,' Mags said in her kindly, no-nonsense way, and put out her hand. Ellie resigned herself to her fate and came.

That was when Mags saw Winnie, sitting quietly at the end of the waiting area, gazing out through the window. There was something so sad and resigned about the way she was sitting there that Mags grew thoughtful. Winnie hadn't seen her. Mags hesitated, wondering whether she should speak to the old woman. But Ellie was looking up at Mags curiously, waiting, and Mags decided against it, and instead to get Ellie back to the ward and her big farewell.

In the Isolation Unit, Kieran told a groggy Matt: 'We're running some tests on your sputum – that's the stuff you've been coughing up. It could take a while for the tests to come through, so you're going to have to bear with us.'

Matt was dismayed. 'Do I have to stay in here?'

''Fraid so. We're concerned that what you've got

might be contagious. So no visitors, either, unless they're relatives. But then you haven't got any, have you?'

Matt looked panicky. He'd been so delirious last night, he couldn't remember what he'd said and what he hadn't. But if they let in relatives . . .

He said, 'Yes, Winnie's my gran. She came with me in the ambulance . . .'

Kieran was surprised. 'She never said last night . . .'

'I want to see her. She came before, but they wouldn't let her in.'

'Well, that was because we didn't know. Of course you can see her if she's your gran. We thought you were sleeping rough –'

Matt asked quickly: 'You haven't been on to Social Services, have you? 'Cos there's no need, I'm living with my gran.'

Kieran too had suddenly thought of something, and he was looking concerned, for a different reason from the one Matt was fearing. 'How long have you been living with your gran?'

Kieran went straight up to the ward and had a word with Sandra Mitchell. 'That old lady who brought Matt in last night. There's a strong chance that she'll have been infected. Turns out he's been in close contact with her – living with her. She's his gran. She needs to be contacted.'

Mags, near by, overheard. 'No need! I've just seen her, down the corridor.' She added, puzzled, 'She's not his gran, though. She was here this morning, and I asked her if she was a relative and she said no.' They all shrugged. 'Anyway,' Mags concluded, 'you don't sit around a hospital half the morning worrying about someone you don't know, do you?' And Kieran went off to look for her.

She was nowhere to be found. She had disappeared.

Sandra Mitchell had been on to Social Services. 'They've got a file on him as long as your arm. Been in care since his parents died when he was five. Disappeared from his last foster home about three months ago. No record of any grandparents.' Winnie wasn't Matt's gran.

But Kieran was still anxious to trace her. 'She needs to have a TB test, and the sooner the better.' He showed them a crumpled piece of paper. 'Got her address off the ambulance people.'

Sandra looked down her nose at him coolly. 'It's not our responsibility.'

Mags took the paper from Kieran and looked at it. 'She only lives ten minutes away on the bus. Why doesn't someone pop round?'

Sandra sighed impatiently. 'I don't like my staff wading in unofficially.' There had already been too much of that, Sandra thought privately, thinking back to her own scrape with Cath Wilson. She said in a heartfelt way, 'You don't know what you're getting into, for one thing.'

But, of course, Mags and Kieran knew nothing about all that, and Mags had a bee in her bonnet by now. 'Look. All I know is, I saw a very worried little old lady in here earlier –'

Kieran persisted in backing her up. 'Come on, Sandra, we've scared her off, we could wait for ever for her to turn up again.'

Mags looked at Sandra's intractable face. Then she said in an exaggeratedly casual tone: 'Well, I suppose what I do in my dinner-break is my own business.' And she pocketed the note.

Mags looked round the musty-smelling living room as Winnie poured the tea. Winnie was confessing to her how she had stumbled over Matt outside the supermarket. He'd got up and helped her across the road. As she took his arm she'd noticed how thin he was. She had invited him home for some dinner. And after that, whenever things got too bad for him, he'd kept coming back . . . He had said to her, 'Can't you adopt me, Winnie?' and she'd had to reply, 'It's me that's the one who needs to be adopted.'

'It's my eyes, you see,' she told Mags. 'I can't see like I used to. That's why everything's so dirty. I can't do stuff like I used to.' She sighed. 'I know what'll happen if anyone starts making inquiries.'

Mags surveyed the room. No, Social Services would never allow it. Winnie could barely look after herself, never mind a tubercular fifteen-year-old boy. Even if there weren't others with more legal claims to him . . .

Mags took a breath. She said gently: 'They've already made inquiries, love.'

Winnie was desperate. She wrung her hankie in her hand. 'They're going to take him away again, aren't they? I won't be able to see him.' She looked at Mags anxiously. 'Is he going to be all right?'

'It isn't just Matt we're worried about, love. We don't know how long Matt has had TB. And if he's been staying with you off and on . . . We want you to come to the chest clinic first thing in the morning.'

Mags and Keely were stacking the tea-trolley. Near by, Martin the decorator passed Sandra Mitchell and gave her a mocking formal salute which Sandra chose to ignore. Mags was surprised to see Keely grinning at Martin, appreciating this joke at another person's expense. Mags scowled, showing that she didn't think it very funny herself. One person's good joke could be another person's bad one. 'Proper little caution, isn't he?' she remarked drily.

Keely seemed unaware of Mags's disapproval.

'He's asked me out,' she said, trying to sound casual, but not without a hint of excitement.

Now Mags really did disapprove.

Keely saw her expression. 'He knows about Billy!' she protested, defensive and rattled. 'It's only for a drink and a laugh.'

'Huh!' said Mags and turned away, leaving Keely offended. As if she couldn't handle it and keep it in perspective . . .

Swifty had come in with Tom and was chatting to Natalie. He was telling her about all the times he'd been in as a patient, listing them off on his fingers.

She laughed. 'Well, look on the bright side. At least your mum's a nurse . . .'

'Eh?'

'Sister Mitchell. Isn't she your mum?'

Something funny then happened to Swifty. As soon as Natalie said it, he came over all pleased at the thought of Sandra being his mum. He could feel his cheeks going red with pleasure. And yes, he thought, in a way Sandra was already almost his mum. The next step seemed pretty obvious . . .

'No,' he told Natalie. 'She's my dad's girlfriend. They're not married. But they soon will be.'

After lights-out, Natalie couldn't sleep, and Nurse Gallagher came for a chat.

Natalie asked her, 'When's Sister Mitchell's wedding?'

'What?' Diane sat back, amazed.

'Swifty told me. It's all arranged.'

Eleven o'clock, and Martin and Keely were walking back from the pizza restaurant.

Keely was getting uneasy. They'd had a good laugh, and the evening had been easy, but as they neared her house, Martin had grown intent. She went up the step to the door. 'I'd ask you in for coffee, but I've to be in at seven tomorrow.'

He smiled. 'I don't want any coffee.' But he came up the step towards her, nevertheless. 'Don't I get a kiss?'

She laughed awkwardly: she didn't know how to take it, what he meant by it.

She went to give him a quick, light peck on the cheek. Before she knew it, he was kissing her properly, passionately, and before she knew it, she was responding.

She pulled away. 'No –'

He tried to pull her back to him. 'Keely –'

'No, I love Billy! I thought you understood, Martin –'

He stared at her, thwarted and offended. There was no understanding in his gaze, if anything, he was angry. He turned on his heel and walked away.

Ten

'Big day for you, Jude,' Diane remarked to him next morning. Today Jude was to be moved to the Rehabilitation Unit, where he would stay for six weeks before finally going home. There he would continue to be taught basic skills, and in the meantime the Latimers' house was to be converted to accommodate him, with a downstairs lavatory and a chair lift on the stairs.

'Yup,' Rob answered for him. 'Mum and Dad are due any time.'

Jude gazed affectionately at Rob, to whom he'd grown attached during his time here in the hospital, though there was no way of guessing how much he understood of what Rob was saying now.

Observing from near by, Mags shook her head. What a waste, she was thinking.

But then something happened to brighten her up. Diane turned to Rob and asked, eager and conspiratorial: 'Have you heard?'

'What?'

'Mitchell's getting married.'

Mags was over like a shot. Nothing she liked better than a good bit of gossip, and this was amazing news indeed.

Diane rolled her eyes. 'Can't keep anything secret on this ward, can you?'

'To Tom?' Rob was asking, and Diane nodded.

'She told you?' Mags wanted to know.

'No, Swifty told Natalie.'

'Oh-ho,' Mags grinned gleefully. 'She's a dark horse! When is it?'

'I don't know. She hasn't confided in me.' And, if truth were told, Diane was a little offended by that.

And then they saw Sandra Mitchell herself coming down the ward towards them. 'Mags!' she called.

'Don't say anything!' Diane warned under her breath.

'Mags,' Sandra was asking her, 'Pharmacy has sent the wrong drugs. Can you take them back and change them?'

'Certainly!' Mags grinned in such a knowing and significant way that Sandra looked at her in puzzlement.

Privately, Diane rolled her eyes again.

As Mags made her way towards the office to collect the drugs for Pharmacy, Keely was coming in the opposite direction, bringing a patient back from X-ray.

Keely approached the ward and saw with embarrassment that Martin was ahead with his mate in the corridor, beginning to sand down some woodwork. It would be their first encounter since the doorstep incident last night. She saw that he had seen her coming and had turned away, pretending he hadn't. As she got level, he kept his back turned, but the moment she'd passed his mate gave an insolent, knowing laugh.

She prickled all over with hurt and shame. And anger: so that's what you had to expect if all you wanted was a bit of light-hearted company when you were lonely: to be the butt of snidey, sexist male jokes.

At that moment Mags reached her, grinning. ''Ey, guess what?'

'What?' Keely's tone was hostile, and she didn't stop, only slowed down. She was in no mood to find anything funny.

Mags was too full of the news to notice. She nodded back towards Sandra, who was disappearing into the office. 'Wedding bells. Her and Swifty's dad.'

Keely was at least surprised, and faintly interested. But she was still walking backwards and, before Mags could warn her it was a secret, she bumped into Rob.

'Sorry –' she began; but he was glaring disapprovingly, so she returned his hostility and swept on.

In the ward entrance she met Diane. ''Ey, have you heard –?' Diane began.

'Yeah, and I hope they'll be dead happy together,' Keely snapped, leaving Diane wondering what on earth was eating her.

Sandra Mitchell was looking thoughtfully through Matt's file.

'Listen to this,' she said suddenly to Mags, who was in the office picking up the drugs. 'In 1992 he attacked one of his foster parents with a broken bottle.' She read on, skimming through. 'He seems quite fond of violence. Countless shoplifting offences . . .' She picked out key words as she read. 'Unmanageable . . . uncontrollable . . . difficult to handle.'

Mags was bemused. 'Well, you wouldn't think you were describing the same lad! Not the way Winnie was talking about him yesterday. She didn't have a bad word to say for him.'

'Really,' Sandra mused, somewhat drily. Her inclination was to believe the notes, rather than Mags's homespun opinion.

Mags shrugged. 'Well, different people see different things, I suppose.' She grinned suddenly and mischievously and said with heavy emphasis: 'It's the same with *love*.'

'What?' Now it was Sandra's turn to be bemused.

Mags giggled, hoping to lead her on to a confession. 'Well, it wouldn't do if we all fancied the same sort, would it?'

'No . . .' What on earth was Mags whittling on about?

Sandra returned to the file, impatient and preoccupied.

But Mags was persisting in her trivial chatter. 'Did you have a nice lunch with *Tom* yesterday?'

Sandra looked up, suddenly interested. 'No! He brought Sean with him!'

'You'll get used to him,' Mags grinned.

'I don't *want* to get used to him!' Sandra was serious. She'd grown very fond of Sean of late, but he really had been a handful. She'd had quite enough of parenthood for the moment. She could do with a rest.

Mags thought this was a joke and went off beaming.

Sandra stared after her curiously.

Kieran had studied Matt's notes, and he did indeed observe that, now that Matt was stronger today, there was a certain belligerence in his attitude.

He asked Kieran roughly: 'Is my gran going to be allowed in to see me?'

'Winnie,' said Kieran carefully. 'Matt, we know she's not your gran.'

Matt clenched his fists, alarmed and angry. 'Have you been on to Social Services?'

Kieran didn't answer straight away. 'All I'm interested in right now is seeing you take it easy –'

Matt interrupted, seeing through his bluff: 'They're always sticking their noses in. Putting me places I don't want to be – stupid, stuck-up families, thinking they're doing me a favour, all *nice* and *understanding*, but they talk to me like I'm not there.' He bashed his fist on his pillow. 'I *knew* this would happen! I *told* her not to ring you!' He glared at Kieran with hatred. 'Why did you have to tell Social Services?'

Kieran told him. 'We're obliged to. It's the law.'

Now a coughing fit seized Matt, and for a moment or two he was unable to say anything. When he finally spoke, his eyes were glittering with intent. 'I want to see her. I want to see Winnie.

'She needs me,' he said quickly, catching Kieran's watchful expression.

It was only minutes after Kieran had gone that Matt struggled weakly out of bed, pulling out his drip. He opened his locker and got his clothes out. For a moment a coughing fit took him. When it was over, he pulled his clothes on, over his pyjamas.

As Mags neared Pharmacy, Matt reached the main corridor. He saw her coming and pulled back round the corner. Mags swished on, unawares, and

Matt crept out again and made it through the hospital doors . . .

Keely was at the end of her tether. A little girl tossed all the pieces of a jigsaw puzzle into the air, and Keely cried loudly, 'What a stupid thing to do! You can just pick them up!'

Everyone turned and stared. Rob came over quickly. Keeping his voice down, in deliberate contrast to hers, he told her, 'There's no need to shout. She didn't do it on purpose –'

Keely cut him off angrily. 'Oh, well, if you know so much, you can help her pick them up.' And she stamped away.

The little girl gazed after her and then, in awed interest at this staff squabble, watched Rob patiently start to pick the pieces up.

Diane had seen it all and, determined, she set off out of the ward after Keely.

She caught up with her at the office. Keely was just in the doorway asking Sandra Mitchell if she could go for her break. 'Keely, can I have a word?'

Keely glanced back sullenly: 'Yeah –' and she put her head back into the office. 'Oh,' she said to Sandra, somewhat ungraciously. 'Congratulations.'

Sandra looked up in bewilderment. 'On what?'

'On getting married.'

Sandra's mouth dropped open as Diane drew Keely back out again and the door shut behind her.

Diane looked at Keely grimly. 'A word about *professionalism.* You shouldn't speak to another member of staff like that in front of the patients.'

Keely was furious. 'Well, I'm sick of it. Just 'cos I passed and he didn't. *He* was the one deliberately embarrassing *me* in front of the patients!'

The door opened behind them.

Sandra asked, 'What's going on?'

They both shut up, Keely still fuming.

Sandra assessed the situation quickly. 'Go for your break, Keely,' she said calmly. 'And then I want to see you and Rob, here.'

Diane was rattled. Now who was publicly undermining someone else's authority?

Then they were both shaken out of their hurt pride when Sandra asked with genuine puzzlement: 'Why am I being congratulated on getting married?'

Keely shrugged foolishly. 'I thought you were.'

'Well, I'm not. At least, as far as I'm aware, I'm not. Maybe you'd like to tell everyone.'

Mags came huffing along the corridor. 'Matt's disappeared!'

Anne Harris, the Social Worker, was called and came immediately to the Children's Ward office.

Kieran was certain that Matt would have gone back to Winnie's.

Sandra Mitchell was dubious. 'He'd know that that's the first place we'd look.' Having looked at his file, she felt he was someone to be reckoned with.

Anne Harris shook her head. 'He mightn't be thinking logically. He might be panicking.'

They all looked at one another. And with his history of violence . . . The old lady trusted him implicitly, she seemed even to love him, but she gave an impression of being quite confused, and as far as Matt was concerned she was probably just a soft touch . . .

Anne looked at Sandra and Kieran. 'So do you want the police involved?'

Kieran hesitated. If he encouraged Anne to go alone to look for Matt at Winnie's, then he could be putting her in danger, too. And yet . . . He wasn't so sure about the danger . . . It was something Matt had said to him . . .

He hesitated long enough for Anne to make the decision to go alone.

Anne knocked at Winnie's back door. She'd already tried the front. All was silent, but she felt sure that they were inside. What did the silence mean? Why was Winnie not answering?

Anne was beginning to get worried.

She peered through the kitchen window. On a work surface was a kettle, a faint wisp of steam curling up from its spout. Someone had boiled it before all went suddenly quiet. She went round to the front again and called through the letter box. 'Winnie! I've come from the hospital! I'm looking for Matt. He's dangerously ill.'

They *were* inside. Winnie was whispering: 'Listen to me, Matt. I had to go in for a test this morning. In case I've got what you've got. TB.'

But Matt was sitting tensely listening to Anne.

Winnie urged, 'Matt, it's serious. People died from it when I was young. I'm so worried about you. You need to go back to hospital. We should answer the door.'

He was silent, so she made her own decision and got up to answer it. He grabbed her wrist and stopped her. 'No!' he hissed intently.

Outside, Anne gave up for the moment. She thought for a while, then made her way across the road to a phone box and rang B1. 'Can you get me a phone number for Winnie?' she asked.

They were in luck. The chest clinic had got Winnie's phone number from her that morning. Kieran scribbled it down on the inside cover of Matt's file. As he was doing so, he noticed Matt's birth date. In one week's time Matt would be sixteen. And Social Services would have no control over him any more . . .

Kieran tapped out Winnie's number.

*

Matt froze as the phone rang. With difficulty, Winnie began to push herself up to answer it.

Matt cried, 'No – !'

Winnie pleaded, 'But, Matt, I'm frightened! You could die if you're not treated!'

The phone went on ringing.

Outside, Anne could hear it, going on and on. Then it suddenly stopped, at the same moment that Anne heard Matt roar, 'No!'

In the hospital, Kieran heard the line go dead.

There was a horrible moment while Anne was imagining what had happened, then she started banging wildly on the door.

It opened. Winnie was standing there worriedly, and behind her in the hall Matt was coughing, over and over, on his hands and knees on the floor. Winnie hurried back to him and bent to help him.

The fit subsided. Anne watched as Winnie embraced him, and Matt laid his poor head in relief on her motherly old shoulder.

Kieran was chuffed. He *knew* he'd been right to believe in Matt. It was when Matt had leant towards him and told him that Winnie needed him. His instinct had told him that Matt meant it. They needed each other, Matt and Winnie; they cared about each other, for all the world like grandson and gran.

And even at this moment, back in his bed on the Isolation Ward, Matt was asking anxiously: 'What about that test Winnie had this morning?'

'Negative.'

Matt grinned in relief.

Kieran asked him: 'So didn't you didn't realize that Social Services will be off your back once you're sixteen?'

Matt shook his head, grinning sheepishly.

In one week's time, long before Matt would be released from the hospital, he would be free to live wherever he liked. Settle down with whomever he decided he wanted to be his gran . . .

Kieran nudged Matt matily and left him.

He went off down the corridor, grinning. About time there was a happy ending. And about time his faith in his own judgement was restored.

Sandra Mitchell was working on another happy ending.

She opened her door on Rob and Keely, who were waiting outside for all the world like two naughty schoolkids up before the Head.

She couldn't help smiling. 'Can you two settle your differences, please? And preferably *not* in front of the children.' It was quite funny really. First the kids fighting and needing to be sorted, and now the staff . . .

Neither of them saw it as remotely like anything

to smile at. They nodded and glanced at each other sullenly.

As Rob made for the door, he remembered. 'Oh, congratulations. By the way.'

She sighed. 'It's only a rumour, Rob.'

He was embarrassed. 'Oh!'

He and Keely made their exits separately and hurriedly, avoiding each other's eyes. It didn't look as though the matter would be settled that easily after all.

A few minutes later, however, Rob followed Keely into the linen room. He said awkwardly, 'I'm sorry, Keely.' He paused, then added: 'But only if you are.'

It was meant to be a joke to break the ice, but Keely didn't seem to get it. 'Yeah . . .' she answered, nodding seriously, and it was then he realized that she was crying.

He came over to comfort her, already forgetting their feud and falling back into old habits. 'What's the matter?'

She turned to him in relief, with her old, habitual, crumpled expression. 'Me! Making a mess of everything! As usual!'

'Come on, tell me.' He started helping her with the linen, working rhythmically alongside her in their old, habitual way.

And so she told him: all about missing Billy, and that awful business with Martin.

When she'd finished, she looked at him anxiously. 'I didn't lead him on. But Mags *told* me not to go. It was really stupid, wasn't it?'

He thought about it seriously, and she waited for his verdict. Then he shook his head. 'No. He's the one who should feel stupid.'

She smiled at him gratefully. It was such a relief to get Rob back as a friend!

The door swung in. Speak of the devil. Martin had seen Keely go in there and had got impatient, waiting for her to come out. 'Can I talk to you, Keely?'

'She's busy,' Rob said quickly and protectively.

Martin tensed with irritation. 'I wasn't talking to you.' He turned to Keely and said derisively, 'You spent most of last night complaining about him.'

Keely said quickly, 'Yeah, well, he probably spent most of last night complaining about *me*.'

Martin faltered at the unexpected solidarity between them, and their joint antagonism towards himself. 'Well,' he mumbled unhappily, surprising them both, 'I wanted to say sorry.'

'Oh . . . right.' Keely looked at the floor, embarrassed, as he left.

Rob and Keely came out of the linen room.

Sandra Mitchell called her, noting their reconciliation and smiling with satisfaction. 'Keely, there was a message for you. From Billy. He's got a few days off. He's arriving to pick you up after work.'

And if they hadn't been in front of the patients, Keely would have flung her arms round Rob with joy.

One person's happy ending can be another's unhappy one. Martin overheard Keely's news with a tug of jealousy and sadness. And then there were Natalie and Wiggy and Mel. Mel and Wiggy had gone home yesterday, and today Wiggy – or, rather, Stephen – was visiting Natalie with a bunch of flowers that looked suspiciously like the ones growing in the park near by.

They were just settling to a game of chess when Mel arrived. She stood in the doorway, in her vivid make-up and her leather coat, and screamed like the Wicked Queen: 'I *knew* you were coming here!' and then she bore down on him and began hitting him.

'Get off him!' Natalie cried, pitching in and bashing at Mel: 'Pick on someone your own size!'

Wiggy looked offended in spite of himself, and Mel roared, and Rob came running to separate them all.

He tried to hold them back, but they went on lunging at one another.

'Pack it in!' he bawled furiously, and Keely tut-tutted him, mocking him cheerfully for shouting at the patients after all.

Sandra told Tom wryly, 'Seems like you and I were

the only ones who didn't know we were getting married.'

He looked at her shyly. 'Seems a shame to disappoint them.'

She stared, first in surprise, then in thoughtful amusement.

He said, 'We're not, are we?'

Her amusement grew. If this was a proposal, then trust Tom to make it the least decisive one in history.

She said gently but firmly, 'No.'

'Oh,' he said, resigned but cheery. He might not be decisive, but he wouldn't give up that easily, after all.

'Anyway,' she reminded him, 'the point is, someone must have put it about.'

They guessed who, and agreed between them to put him right.

That evening, Tom and Sean were due to move out of Sandra's and back to their own house. She arrived home to find them just finishing packing their things in the car.

'Have you told him?' she asked Tom.

'Er . . . no.' Tom was clearly reluctant to do so.

'Told me what?' Swifty was all excitement and expectation.

Tom did so quickly: 'We're not getting married.'

Swifty's grin fell. 'Not?' He looked from one to the other. 'Aw!'

And then he watched Tom and Sandra kissing goodbye and decided that this wasn't the end of it, by any means. There'd be a happy outcome yet . . .

Leanne was determined not to let what had happened to her brother be a tragedy.

She had decorated his room in the Rehabilitation Unit just the way he'd had his room at home, with all the posters crooked instead of straight.

She stayed behind there with him while their mother went to supervise the men who were doing the conversions at home. While the staff took him for his exercises, she busied herself tidying his tapes, and when they brought him back she sat and read to him from *Viz*. But her heart was heavy. He used to crack up, laughing at the jokes, and now he just gazed at her fondly as she read.

There was a movement in the doorway, and Jude grunted in recognition. Leanne looked up. It was Sarah. Leanne jumped up, delighted. She had *told* him he had lots of friends to come and visit . . . and she herself was needing to go to the toilet, and now he had someone to sit with him while she did.

Sarah looked at Jude in revulsion. When he had grunted at her like that, she had jumped; she had felt as though something horrible like an insect had touched her. She knew she shouldn't feel like that, but she did. He was gazing at her now, making little gurgling squeals and dribbling out of the side of his mouth. She shuddered.

Leanne was asking her to sit with him while she went to the toilet. 'Read to him,' she was instructing, encouraging Sarah, handing her the magazine, almost as if showing her how, turning herself into the little motherly nurse.

Sarah sat miserably on the chair Leanne had vacated.

When Leanne came back, Sarah was sitting leafing silently and listlessly through the magazine. Jude was staring into space at her side. For all he seemed to be aware of her, she might as well not have been there.

Leanne was dismayed. 'Why didn't you read to him?' She immediately busied herself in making it up to Jude, giving him a drink.

'Because it doesn't make any difference.' Sarah watched Leanne put the beaker to Jude's lips. The beaker flashed in the sun that was streaming in through the unit window. Liquid spilled, glistening, down the side of his face.

'Faye was right,' she said bitterly. She stood and ran out of the room and the unit, ignoring Leanne's cries.

Leanne stood with her lower lip trembling, understanding that Jude had lost all his friends.

Except herself. He still had her. Determinedly,

she put a smile on her face and went back in to Jude.

Sarah kept running until she got to the park. Then she slowed.

Someone called her name. It was Dan. She looked up. He was messing about at the swings with some lads she didn't know.

He came over. He was cool, he'd got over the shock of being charged, it seemed.

'Who are those lot?' she asked him.

'Some new mates of Faye's.'

'Oh,' she said coldly. 'Still knocking round with her, then?' She made a move. 'See you.'

He came after her. 'Wait –'

She stopped and waited unwillingly. 'What?'

'I don't want to be with Faye. I want to go out with you –'

She interrupted him. 'I've just been to see Jude in the Rehabilitation Unit.'

He didn't get the point. 'Oh yeah?'

She was silent, thinking about it, and then she said, half to herself, 'It wasn't him. It isn't Jude. He's gone, just like Phil.'

As she thought it, a car came screeching into the drive near by, just as it had that day when Jude was damaged, banished for ever . . .

Dan was saying. 'Will you go out with me?' and she realized that it was an ultimatum.

The people in the car were swigging cider and calling him; there were two lads, and Faye was with them.

If she didn't agree, he was going to go with them.

'Don't,' she begged him.

In the background Faye was calling, 'Are you coming, Dan?'

'So will you go out with me?'

She couldn't agree to that, not the way she felt about him now. But she desperately wanted him not to get in the car. 'Don't get in it!'

Faye called, 'Take no notice of her, Dan! She's a little Goody-two-shoes!'

Dan asked, 'Well?'

She couldn't do it. 'Don't go.'

He turned and vaulted the fence, using his good arm, and got into the car.

The lad driving it revved. Faye handed Dan the bottle of cider, and it flashed in the sun like a dangerous signal as he lifted it to his face. Sarah thought of the flashing beaker being lifted to Jude's, and she shut her eyes.

When she opened them again, the gang was screaming off down the road, leaving a trail of dust behind them.

Well, Sarah wouldn't forget. She wouldn't pretend that nothing had happened. She turned away.

Suddenly determined, she set off towards home, to face up to real life.

Some Other Puffins

WOOF! THE NEVER-ENDING TALE

Terrance Dicks

Rex Thomas is a boy. Rex Thomas is a dog. The thing is, he can change between the two at any time. One minute he's lying in bed, the next he's sniffing around his bedroom as a small shaggy mongrel with large brown eyes. Fortunately for Rex, his best friend Michael Tully can help him get out of the stickiest of situations.

Even so, when some 'dog therapy' is required for the local milkman, who better to use than Rex? And when Great Demento the Magician loses his canine assistant Cyril, there's only one dog who can take his place. Life for Rex the boy is always eventful – life for the dog is always an adventure.

FREE WILLY

A novelization by Todd Strasser

Willy is a mighty killer whale. Jesse is an eleven-year-old runaway who never had a real home. Together they form a very special friendship.

The star attraction at an amusement park, Willy is restless and longs to be reunited with his family at sea. The park owner, however, has decided that the whale is worth more dead than alive. Can Jesse free Willy before it's too late?

Madame Doubtfire

Anne Fine

'A vast apparition towered over her on the doorstep. It wore a loose salmon pink coat . . . and tucked under its arm was an enormous imitation crocodile skin handbag . . . "I'm Madame Doubtfire, dear."'

Lydia, Christopher and Natalie Hilliard are used to domestic turmoil and have been torn between their warring parents ever since the divorce. But all that changes when their mother takes on a most unusual cleaning lady.

Despite her extraordinary appearance, Madame Doubtfire turns out to be a talented and efficient housekeeper and, for a short time at least, the arrangement is a resounding success. But, as the Hilliard children soon discover, there's more to Madame Doubtfire than domestic talents . . .

Baby's Day Out

Ron Fontes and Justine Korman

Of all the babies in all the world, they had to pick this one.

It's a beautiful morning in a perfect suburb. An ideal day to arrive at the Cotwells' family home to take photographs of their gorgeous baby boy. After that, it's a simple matter of a few pictures and then a scheme that could make these phoney photographers millions.

What could go wrong? they thought. How could an eighteen-month-old kid possibly outwit us? they said. But then, they hadn't met Baby Bink, and his day out is just about to begin.

The Pagemaster

A novelization by Todd Strasser

Imagine meeting Long John Silver, Dr Jekyll and Moby Dick — in one day!

Richard Tyler is the world's most cautious kid. Fearful of accidents wherever he turns, Richard's greatest fear becomes reality when he gets caught in a freak thunderstorm. He crashes his bike (with extra-special safety features) and rushes for cover into his local library.

There he meets the mysterious Pagemaster who takes him into a fantasy world where books literally come to life. It's not a journey for the faint-hearted, but through it Richard develops a new confidence in himself and the world around him.

Based on the film *The Pagemaster* starring Macaulay Culkin.

Beethoven's 2nd

A novelization by Robert Tine

The Newton family are quite happy as dog people. But never in a million years did George Newton think they would be puppy people.

Enter Beethoven, followed by his friend, Missy, and their four St Bernard puppies. They are cuter than cute and messier than anything. None the less, just like Beethoven, George and his family quickly grow to love them all.

It's a big thing to look after so many dogs. It's an even bigger thing when there are nasty people around who want to put the puppies into breeding kennels, which means it's down to Beethoven and George to save the day!